AWAKENING

AWAKENING

LUCY WALLACE

Palmetto
PUBLISHING GROUP

Palmetto Publishing Group, LLC
Charleston, SC

For information regarding special discounts for bulk purchases, please
contact Palmetto Publishing Group at Info@PalmettoPublishingGroup.com.

ISBN-13: 978-1-944313-76-0
ISBN-10: 1-944313-76-1

For my most valuable treasures,
William and Sammy,
their courage and strength are my inspiration.

CHAPTER
ONE

I LOOK DEEP WITHIN AND THINGS SEEM DARK. It is said that it is darkest before dawn. Could this be the dawning of the new me? Though I have been through some dark times, I have never seen such a dark place like this. I fear what I was before, but fear so much more what is on the horizon. My life has hung in the balance many times. I haven't known whether I would survive each battle or traumatizing trial I have faced. Each time taking a little longer picking myself up and dusting off the horrific events.

I remember having dreams as a child of having complete, unwavering control of every aspect of my life. I have yet to possess that type of control. I have grown up believing I must control my emotions, and detach myself from life. This has been the key to surviving day by day. Each mission has taken a small piece of the person I once was, and replaced it with pure emptiness.

"This is the last one." I vowed to the reflection in the mirror. I hardly recognize the person staring back at me. Their eyes zoned in like lasers, and shimmering like emerald stars with hints of metallic blue glitter floating in the atmosphere. "You can do this, Val." I said as my index finger brushed the scar above my right eyebrow, sparking memories of one of my first missions.

—∿∿—

Victor Santana was my first target. I tracked him all over the lower half of South America, until I finally caught up with him. First, in a warehouse at the Port of Ushaia, South America, where I was captured and left to be tortured, questioned, and finally disposed of by Victor's head of security.

The last thing I remember before waking up tied by my wrists to a steel beam above my head, was being crouched on my perch with my long-range rifle. I was observing Victor conduct business when the butt end of an AK-47 cracked the right side of my head just above my right eye. Lightning from the impact shot through my head, and all went dark.

"Find out what she knows, then get rid of her!"

"Yes, sir!"

As my head was pounding like I'd been on a month-long binder, I could feel the immense swelling in my right eye and the warmth of my blood flowing down the side of my face. You could almost hear the audible sound of the drips as they made contact with and formed a puddle on the sawdust covered cement below my feet. A violent slap to the face was meant as my encouragement to return to the awakened world.

"Alright, honey. Come on back." His name was Bjorn (The Bear) Dervishi. He absolutely lived up to the name 'The Bear', as his build rivaled that of Vin Diesel and The Rock put together. His hair was the color of the sun on a warm spring day, and the glow from it was just as bright.

While firmly gripping my chin with one hand and trailing every inch of my neck with the knife in his other, he pulled me face to face with him and said, "Now, who sent you?"

His voice matched his dominant appearance. The sound

echoed throughout the warehouse causing shivers to race down my spine, and a feeling of disambiguation to flood my mind as I knew what was coming. I felt searing pain as he pressed the tip of his serrated military knife into my left shoulder, in an attempt to press his questioning further. I couldn't help but let out a grunt as the pain seared through my shoulder.

As he balled up his fist he said, "you will talk. I can promise you that." With that, his fist contacted my left cheek just below my eye. Like a human punching bag, the blow caused me to swing by my wrist.

As I recovered from the blow, a smirk appeared on my face. "Oh please, please don't hurt me." I said as I painfully squinted my eyes showing a face of pure defiance, vindictiveness and contemplation. I knew I had to finish this and catch up with Victor in order to complete my mission. All I needed was Bear's military knife to get out of the ropes. I just needed him to finish what he started with my shoulder.

My goal now was to use his frustration against him in order to escape my predicament. He walked over to a nearby table where he removed a cloth revealing a variety of whipping sticks, leather whips, and tasers. "This is going to get messy." I thought to myself.

His weapon of choice the cattle prod he was caressing with his fingers. "Let's see what fifty thousand volts will do to get that mouth of yours to start talking."

I tried not to show the small hint of fear that quickly shot through my body as he slowly walked back over to me with the cattle prod in one hand; while using it to pat his other hand as if he were holding a baseball bat.

Just as I clenched my fists, I was hit with the full force of the fifty thousand volts of electricity from the cattle prod. I couldn't stop the scream that escaped my lips as he held the prod to my sternum, sending pulses of electricity throughout my body. It seemed like an eternity before he removed the prod and asked again, "Now, who sent you?"

Keeping with my plans, I looked him straight in the eyes with a smile growing ever larger on my lips and said, "Ya.....you're going to have to do better than that." The chuckles that escaped from deep in my chest only adding fuel to the ever-growing fire within him. I could see the anger boiling over him. His face turned red with frustration and anger, then began to contort to show the fullness of the emotion.

I was not quite prepared for the onslaught of punches that rattled my stomach and ribs. No amount of training could prepare you for the number of ribs that were broken from the force of the blows they received. It seemed my plan was working a little too well. So far all I've gained was a hard time breathing. "Shit! I need that knife!"

I slowly raised my eyes to meet his and said, "You hit like a girl."

I painfully chuckled at the insult causing his anger level to rise more. My secret prayers were answered as he quickly pulled the knife from its sheath, plunged it to the hilt just below my left shoulder, causing my screams to echo throughout the warehouse. That hurt like hell as it crushed through bone and muscle.

I felt myself beginning to black out from the pain as he turned to walk back over to the table. I knew I had to fight through the pain as this was my chance to get free while his back was turned. I grit my teeth as I slowly pulled my body up where I could grab the handle of the knife. While firmly holding the handle, I let my body drop using the force to rip the knife from my chest. Once free, I used the serrated edge to saw through the rope above my hands. I watched as each strand of the rope broke away, edging me closer to freedom. "Come on, last one." I thought as the knife sawed through the last strand causing me to drop into a crouch on the floor.

"Let's make this quiet." I thought as I freed my hands and began to move toward my current target. I cunningly moved toward 'Bear' using stealth like footsteps to avoid being caught. I gripped the handle of the knife in my right hand and like a bullet from a gun, I lunged myself toward his back. My left hand wrapped around his head and firmly gripped the right side of his face while I plunged the knife into the carotid artery on the left side of his neck. The knife slid into his neck as if it were cutting into butter. With as much force as I could muster, I quickly drug the smooth side of the blade through muscle and cartilage; ripping his neck open from artery to artery causing blood to spray over the table and its contents. After a few moments of hearing the bubbling gurgle sounds emanating from him, his body fell bunglingly over the table. I sluggishly slid off of his back, then down to my knees on the floor.

"Damn! This is going slow things down a little." I said to myself as I examined my wounds.

It took me a minute to gather the strength to move again. Needing to stop the bleeding from my shoulder, I looked around the room for something to use as a bandage until I could stitch the two-inch laceration. The only thing I could find was a shop rag laying on a workbench in the corner of the room.

"This will have to do." I said as I tore the cloth in half. I twisted one of the halves, placed it in my mouth, and bit down with it between my teeth. My intention was to use the other half to pack the wound in order to stop the bleeding.

"Ugh! Damn it!" I said through my teeth as I purposely stuffed the cloth into the wound in my shoulder.

"This should help with the bleeding until I can find a needle and thread." I said as I stood up. I used the piece of cloth from my mouth to wipe the blood from the military knife and shoved it into my right boot.

"Now, I need to get out of here and catch up with Victor."

I took a moment to glance out of the small window on the far side of the room to observe my situation. It was lightly guarded, as most of the highly-trained henchmen and bodyguards were with Victor.

"This may be an easy escape." I said as I moved to the only door in the room. It led to the main area of the warehouse where I was being detained.

"Shit!" I whispered under my breath.

The guard at the door had an automatic weapon cradled to his chest ready to use at a moment's notice. He was the only one I saw, but that didn't mean there wouldn't be more. I quietly closed the door back and walked over to the table where "Bear" was obliquely lying, and picked up the bloody cattle prod. I had to re- sist the urge to use it on his enormously large, and extremely dead body. While formulating a plan in my head, I quietly moved back towards the door. I stealthily turned the knob opening the door just enough to get the cattle prod through. I then shoved the prod into the guard's back while pressing the trigger.

"Ugh…." Was the only audible sound the guard made as I followed him down to the ground while still maintaining contact with the cattle prod. Once on the ground stunned, I reach down and unclipped the clasp on the shoulder strap of his automatic weapon; then quickly slammed the butt end of the gun into his head.

Now armed with something better than a cattle prod, I surveyed the rest of the warehouse for more guards. Only finding two at the far end of the warehouse standing next to a small pickup truck. I quietly laid the cattle prod down next to the downed guard and decided to make a silent but hasty exit through the door to my right. To my surprise, this door led to a dock overlooking the port. Not only did I see barrels and crates lining the dock, I also had the glare of the sun as it danced across the water.

"Nice! Lots of cover for an easier escape." I thought to myself as I moved, in a crouched position, towards some barrels. Once there, I thoroughly observed my surroundings.

"So far so good." I said quietly while still crouched by the barrels. I gathered my strength and newly acquired weapon, then made my way to a pile of crates that were a little farther down the dock. From there I had a better view of the two guards standing next to the truck.

"Sorry boys. This isn't going to be fun for either of you." I said as I made my way to the truck at the end of the dock. Some of these idiots don't know how to use a gun, much less fight. My plan was to deal with both of them as quietly as possible in an effort to not raise an alarm.

Although I had a solid plan, things did not go quite the way I expected them to. I used the piles of crates and barrels on the edge of the dock to edge my way closer to the small truck. Once close enough I used the distraction of their obviously riveting conversation to sneak up on the guard closest to me. I grabbed the guard, in the same manner that I did bear when I sliced his neck open; then used him as a shield toward the guard on the other side of the truck. At that point I hurled the knife at the chest of the guard on the other side of the truck. The knife met its mark perfectly as it pierced his chest, making him fall silently to the ground. I then added enough pressure to break the neck of the guard in my arms. I quickly jumped into the driver's seat of the truck and sped away leaving marks tattooed on the pavement as the back tires spun out of control due to the amount of pressure I placed on the accelerator. My main priority was to catch up with Victor, but the injuries I sustained needed attention.

I pulled up to my safe house on the other side of the city of Ushuaia. Once inside, I searched through my things in order to find my med bag. I needed some type of suture material to close the opening in my shoulder.

Finding the materials I needed, I made my way to the bathroom in order to use the mirror to see what I was doing. I first gave myself a quick shot of the morphine from my med pack to take the edge off of the pain.

Before removing the makeshift packing from the wound in my shoulder, I used some lidocaine around the wound to numb the area. Either way I knew this was going to be an extremely painful process.

Once sutured and properly bandaged, I took a moment to go through my notes from the surveillance I had of Victor in order to better calculate my next move. According to my intel, Victor would be headed to his hideout in Brazil before leaving the country. If you could call a mansion on the coast a hideout.

I knew I had to finish this before he had a chance to leave South America. The fastest way to Brazil was by plane, so my next stop was the airport where I had my small plane waiting for me.

Before the wheels were on the ground in Brazil, I already formulated a plan. Victor wasn't going to get away, nor was I going to put myself in the position to be captured again. This was going to end here. For Victor, at least.

My plan was to find some viable cover at a concealed distance from Victor's mansion; where I could finally finish this mission, and return home.

Due to my drive for absolution, there was no need to secure a safe house. I immediately acquired transportation in the form of an off-road vehicle, and made my way toward Casa de Santana.

Luckily, Victor enjoyed seclusion. His home was set off from any main road, and was literally right on the coast. Talk about your beach front property. The lives that these scumbags lived at the expense of their victims made me sick. Yet, that knowledge alone made the execution of my job that much easier; leaving me with little to no remorse over their deaths.

I found a nice wooded patch about five hundred yards from Victor's house that provided an impeccable vantage point. I have to admit; the scenery was absolutely beautiful. Under any other circumstance, I would've loved to sit back and enjoy it.

The warm salty air filled my lungs with each breath, and left a taste of sea spray, the sweetness from nearby flowers, and a hint of Brigadeiro that was being made at a nearby house. The sway of the palm trees as they moved and danced in the breeze was almost relaxing. Even if I wasn't on a mission, I don't think the monster in me would allow me the pleasure of enjoying this seemingly wonderful atmosphere.

Through my rangefinders, I could see Victor sitting in a lounger by the pool. He had a couple of his guards standing next to him, and seemed to be barking orders. His face seemed to turn red with every word that escaped his lips, leaving his guards to robotically hang on everyone. Once their proverbial tongue lashing was over, they excused themselves and seemingly left Victor alone. Little did they all know that I was, however distant, there with him.

I'm not sure why, but I took my time unpacking my rifle. Every move was deliberate as I put the pieces of the rifle together, and finally attached to scope to its mount.

"Time to say goodbye Victor." I said as I slowly pulled a bullet from the sheath of ammo strap on my arm, and used my right forefinger to lightly press on its tip. I slid open the action on the rifle and slid the bullet into place, closing the action behind it. While looking through the high-powered scope, I found my target. I then tweaked the range on the scope until I felt I had him accurately placed within the crosshairs.

As I calculated for the wind speed, Victor was still laid back on the lounger. I took slow calculated breaths so that the rise and fall of my chest would not interfere with my shot as I slowly put pressure on the trigger.

It almost seemed like Victor looked right at me as the rifle went off and sent hot lead racing towards his head. It was only about a second before the force of the bullet sent Victor's head backwards, and sent his arms flying up in an almost 'I don't care' motion before his body went totally limp and lifeless.

———

The beeping from my phone brought me back to the present. It was a message from my handler:

Tá do sprioc Tripp Maseru. Is Sprioc suíomh Linz An Ostair (Your target is Tripp Maseru. Target location is Linz Austria.)

"Great! Looks like another trip around the world." I said as I pulled out my box of fake identities and passports. Digging through all of the various choices, I found my next identity. Ms. Svetlana Romanov. Nothing like an identity to suit the area.

I pulled out the case of money that contained every currency of the world. I not only pulled out fifty thousand in American currency, I also packed another fifty thousand euros. After packing everything that was needed for my trip, I left for my personal airfield to load and fuel my jet. I've found that in my line of work, it's great not having to deal with the headache of commercial airlines.

"Okay Val. This is the last one." I thought to myself as I began my takeoff. My goal was to finish this job then retire and go off the grid. In this line of work, it's never a matter of just retiring. If you want out, you have to be ready to cut and run.

CHAPTER
TWO

TRIPP MASERU, A DIRTY DIPLOMAT, has plans to use drug lords and the mafia to overthrow the government. I have a special kind of hate for people like this. When I was only thirteen, my soul was torn in two when my father and mother were murdered in their small grocery shop by a member of a local gang. My sister, Tara, who was only eleven at the time, and I were sent to an orphanage after that. Over the next few years I lost all parts of the young and happy girl I once was. I learned to replace all traces of that girl with a shell of a person that was the embodiment of emotionless rage. At sixteen I ran away leaving my sister behind. At that point in my life I didn't even care for her.

After landing in Linz I made my way to the Hotel Ibis. The building itself was much like something you would see in a futuristic movie. The front of the building almost looked like it was made of one side of the Louvre.

"Welcome to the Hotel Ibis Linz City. How may I assist you?" The young lady behind the desk said.

"Svetlana Romanov, checking in." I replied.

"Yes Ms. Romanov. We have your room ready. I'll get someone to help with your bags." She said while handing me the key card to my room.

As I walked away from the desk towards the elevators, I looked back and said thank you. In the very same motion I turned back towards the elevators. After pressing the metal button on the wall with the arrow indicating going up, I waited with noticeable impatience.

"In a hurry?" I turned at the remark to see Tripp standing right behind me.

"Damn!" I thought to myself.

Reluctant to engage in the conversation I replied, "Yes, I left my phone in my room, and I am expecting a call."

"I see, but tapping your foot and shaking your hands isn't going to make the elevator move any faster." Was his reply.

I replied with rolling my eyes and turning away from him. I didn't want to have this conversation, especially with him, but damn he was cute! Even more so in person. I didn't need this distraction! I tried to focus my attention on anything else but him.

"Val. Why did mom and dad have to die?"

"I'm not sure, Tara." I said as my heart broke at my sister's pain. "Sometimes bad things just happen." I said while choking back tears.

"We'll always be together, right?" She asked through her tears.

"Yes, Tara. Forever and always."

I swept the tear from my eye as the bell from the elevator indicated its arrival, and the doors opened. I stepped into the elevator, but turned around to see Tripp hovering over the panel of buttons.

"Which floor?" His crystal blue eyes seemed to be reading right into me.

"Thirteen." I replied.

"Looks like we are headed in the same direction." He said with a smile.

"Seems so." I said as I placed my back against the far side of the elevator. I was trying not to let the frustration and irritation over the situation show.

Thanks to this impromptu run in with Tripp, I'm going to need an extra few minutes to mentally prepare for this mission. Leaning back against the elevator wall, I placed my arms across my chest and kept my eyes on the floor in hopes to deter any further pursuance of the conversation on his part.

It was as if time had stood still. The elevator was moving at too slow a pace. Especially since I had an unwanted companion. I was running a little behind schedule with my arrival, and was paying dearly for it now. The temptation to get off at the next floor and take the stairs the rest of the way was a bit overwhelming, but I didn't want to give him a reason to be suspicious about me.

"Finally!" I thought to myself, although the word narrowly escaped my lips, as the elevator buzzed and the doors opened to the thirteenth floor.

Tripp motioned for me to exit first, then followed in suit. I glanced up at the plaque on the wall that indicated the directions for the room numbers, and quickly turned right to make my way to room 1303. Thankfully Tripp walked in the opposite direction.

I pushed the keycard into the door lock, removed it and waited for the green light to flash indicating the lock was opened. I quickly opened the door, walked inside, and locked the door behind me. While making my way to the oversized king bed, I was overcome with emotions I haven't felt since my parents were taken from me.

I slowly sank down on the bed and began to think back to the conversations between Tara and I before I ran away.

———ᴠᴠᴠ———

"Tara, I can't stay here!" I barked out in frustration.

"What are you talking about, Val?" Tears were welling up in her eyes. "I thought we were going to stick together forever and always!" She said as she threw the book she was reading on the bed.

"Tara, I know I said that, but things change. You'll be just fine without me." My anger and frustration was getting the better of me. "Cian will take care of you and watch your back. You don't need me anymore."

"Val, please don't go!" Tara pleaded with me as emotion filled every word.

———ᴠᴠᴠ———

I must have dozed off, because the shimmering of the city lights were playfully passing through the window as the curtains moved with the airflow from the heater under the window.

I slowly heaved myself from the side of the bed closest to the door, and stretched my back, legs, and arms to get the blood flowing once again to my muscles. In order to motivate myself, I decided to clean up before glancing at my itinerary for the evening.

I moved sluggishly toward the small bathroom; my mind and body still slightly overcome by the trip. I wet one of the small wash cloths then used it to wipe my face in an attempt to expedite the process of waking up. I slept entirely too long. It was apparent that my body needed more rest as it resisted each attempt to awaken.

After cleaning up a bit, and vigorously jostling my head in an effort to wake my brain, I decided to sit at the small desk that was situated next to the dresser in my room.

I pulled the file I had for Tripp from my briefcase and began to familiarize myself with my target. I needed to formulate a plan that would get me close enough to him to complete my mission.

Though I normally do not drink while on mission, I decided to see what the mini bar in my room had to offer. I had a cardinal desire to calm my nerves a bit. It was apparent that something here had my mind running wild on me. My memories of the past were being triggered by something in this city or hotel, and I had no clue what or who it was. In the last fifteen years I have never felt the emotions that were beginning to take me over, and I needed to get them back in check. I hadn't thought of my sister, or Cian for that matter, since I left fifteen years ago. So why am I thinking of them now?

"Get a grip, Val!" I condemned myself. "What the hell is going on with me?"

I pulled a small bottle of vodka from the mini fridge and poured it over a small glass of ice. I had to find some way of numbing these memories. Or at the very least burry them again. The emotions that were flooding in because of them were making me feel weak. I haven't felt a sense of weakness since my parents were taken from me and my sister.

CHAPTER
THREE

LYING ON MY BUNK, memories of my parents murders flooded my mind. That night was undeniably the worst night of my life. I remember hearing loud voices from downstairs in my father's shop. He owned a small convenience store of sorts. It had been closing time, and my father was downstairs cleaning the shop and closing things down. I had barely gotten down the stairs that linked our apartment to the shop when I heard my father.

"Please, take whatever you want and leave. Just don't hurt my family." My father's voice was firm, yet contained a hint of fear.

"Oh, you don't understand. We don't want anything from your small shop. We were ordered to kill you and your family." One of the men replied.

"Please, you don't have to do this!" My father pleaded as he was backing up towards the sales counter. I could only imagine that he was making his way towards his handgun.

While watching and listening from the staircase, my heart began to pound with anxiety, making it feel as though it would explode within my chest. As my father reach for his weapon the other guy fired four times with his rather large pistol. Each shot hit its mark leaving two bullet wounds in my father's chest, one in his right shoulder, and the last in his gut. It seemed as though my father was dead before he hit the floor, but as he lay there he moaned in pain for a moment, then let out his last breath with a barely audible gurgle as blood began to fill his lungs.

While standing there, frozen in fear, my mother came downstairs after having heard the gunfire. I felt her hands on my shoulders from behind as she shook me back to reality.

"Val!" She said in a forceful whisper. "Val! Go upstairs and hide with your sister. Do not come out! Do you understand me?"

"Yes ma'am." I said through the tears and fear that seemed to flood over and overwhelm me.

I turned towards my mother, who gave me a quick hug, and quickly made my way back up to our apartment, stumbling up a few of the stairs on my way. The smell of the burnt gunpowder seemed to follow me as I entered the threshold of our home. I ran into the room that my sister, Tara, and I shared, and found her huddled in the corner on the far side of the room. She was crying and shaking uncontrollably. I all but ran over to her and kneeled down to one knee in front of her.

"Tara! We have to go!" I said while wiping tears from my cheeks. "We have to go now!"

"Val, I'm scared." She said in a tearfully shaky voice.

"Me too, Tara. But we have to find somewhere to hide right now." I told her as I grabbed her hand and pulled her to her feet.

I was all but dragging her down the small hallway to our usual hiding place in the small closet of the bathroom. Our apartment was small. There were two bedrooms, a bathroom, a small kitchen where we had a very small table, and a living room. There were very few places to hide, so the bathroom closet had to do. It was hardly big enough for Tara and I. I opened the door and ushered Tara in.

"Come on, Tara. You have to get in!" I told her as I opened

the door to the closet.

As she began to bend down and crawl into the small space, I heard our mother scream and a couple more gun shots. Fear and sorrow gripped me as I knew then that our mother was taken from us. It was that moment that I, in a panic induced rushed, pushed Tara into the closet. I then climbed in the best that I could; closing the door behind us.

I heard heavy footsteps coming up our stairs and a low burly voice say, "make sure there's no one else here. We can't leave witnesses."

"Yeah, yeah." The other guy said. His voice was not as deep. He almost sounded like he was younger. Maybe in his twenties.

As I heard them rummaging through my house anger shot through me like a bullet. It's strange that I wasn't angry at the time about both of my parents being taken from my sister and I. I was angry that there was nothing I could do but hide in this closet and protect my sister. Just as the thought of jumping out and fighting went through my mind, I heard footsteps in the bathroom. I put my hand over my sister's mouth as the handle of the closet door shook. I thought for sure we were caught and would be killed. Just then I heard the burly voice again.

"There's no one here. Come on let's get out of here!" He said.

In a matter of minutes, it seemed as though they were gone. I waited in the cramped closet until I all but lost the feelings in my legs.

"Tara, I'm going to check things out. Stay here until I come back. Don't make a sound!" I told my sister.

"Val, Please, don't leave me here! What if they are still here?" Her voice was shaking from fear.

"Everything will be fine, Tara. Just stay put." I did my best to calm her down as I climbed out of the closet and shut the door behind me.

I glanced at myself in the mirror before opening the bathroom door. It was then that I could see the surge of anger on my face. I used that as motivation as I poked my head out of the door into the hallway. After seeing that no one was there, I eased out into the hall and towards what used to be our living room. There was stuff everywhere.

It was like a tornado tore through my home. The couch and arm chair were flipped over and thrown across the room, the coffee table was broken in two, and everything was pulled from the cabinets in the kitchen. Cleaning up was the last of my worries. My main focus was making sure those men were gone, and checking on my parents.

I eased down the stairs as quietly as possible and found my mother's body lying almost lifeless about half way down. I rushed to her side hoping and praying that she was still alive. As I rolled her over onto her back she looked at me. Her eyes seemed distant, and I knew she was fading fast. It was then that I heard my mother's voice for the last time.

"Valentine, you have to take care of your sister." Her voice was faint and distant. "Promise me you'll watch after her."

"I will." I said while choking back the sobs. "Mom, please don't leave!" I said as I hugged her limp body, then laid my head on her chest. "I need you, mom!"

"You'll be o...k...kay" She said in a whisper. Then she was gone.

"Mom...Mom!" I yelled as I shook her limp and lifeless body. "Mom, Please! Please don't go!" I cried.

I laid my head across her chest again and cried for what seemed like hours. I knew my father was already gone, so I dreadfully made my way back upstairs, making sure to wipe the tears from my eyes and face on the way. I knew I had to get my sister out of here, but had no idea how to get her past all of the carnage within the path of our escape. Leaving only my sister and I behind, all I have ever known was now gone.

Stepping over the broken furniture and glass, I made my way past all of the destruction within my home. I went straight down the hall, past the bathroom, then walked into the bedroom Tara and I shared. My concern at this point was changing out of my blood-stained shirt. I rummaged through our torn-up room and found an old bandana along with a light jacket that was lying on the floor between our beds and put it on. My priority now was to protect Tara. I then briskly walked into the bathroom where Tara was still hiding.

"Tara, it's me." I warned before opening the closet door.

"Val? Val, where's mom and dad?" She asked with a tearful voice.

"Everything's going to be okay, Tara." I hated giving her a broken promise. "I need you to put this over your eyes, okay?" I said as I leaned towards her to wrap the bandana around her head in an attempt to cover her eyes.

"Val, I'm scared."

"I know, Tara. Me too, but we have to get out of here." I spoke with urgency while helping her out of the closet and to her feet.

As she emerged from the closet, she stumbled a little. This was more than likely attributed to being cramped in that small closet for so long, as well as not being able to see from having the bandana over her eyes. I hated that last part, but it seemed necessary in order to get her out of here without insane amounts of hysteria that would undoubtedly ensue from the carnage.

I wrapped my arm under hers to help support her as we navigated our way through the maze of what was left of our home. As we arrived at the top of the stairs I began to worry whether or not Tara could really see through the bandana. Deciding to test her, I raised my hand like I wanted to slap her, and swung it towards her face. Not wanting to really hit her, I stopped just shy of her cheek. The lack of a response let me know it was safe to continue down the stairs.

I started down first, taking each step backwards in an attempt to guide Tara and limit her amount of stumbling. It was at the point of us passing our mother's body that I had to fight the tears and strained to suppress my emotions. I knew from this point on that I needed to become a pillar of strength for my sister.

Once outside I took the bandana off of Tara's eyes and wrapped my arms around her. I knew we would have some very hard times in the days ahead. I loosened my grasp around my sister just enough to look her in the eyes. I could see the pain and devastation welling up within them.

"Val? Mom and dad are gone, aren't they?" She asked as tears began to trickle from her eyes.

I couldn't lie to her. It took all of my inner strength to gain the courage to tell her the truth without allowing my emotions to take control.

There was a war beginning to rage within me. I was fighting a battle between the sadness and devastation of losing my parents, and the anger towards the people who took them from my sister and I. I knew deep down my childhood was now over.

"Yes, Tara." Was all I could say through grit teeth as I began to see red. The anger within me had won the war, and my response sounded more callous than that of a comforting sister. I know I have to keep my promise to my mother, but I wanted revenge so badly I could practically taste it.

The next few hours were a blur as police officers arrived,

wrapped blankets around our shoulders, then escorted my sister and I to the station for questioning.

Tara was an emotional wreck the entire time. I'm almost certain the officers took my lack of emotion as a form of shock from witnessing my parents' deaths; so, I just left it at that. It wasn't long before an older woman from the orphanage showed up to take Tara and I away due to the fact that we had no other family to take care of us.

We seemed to drive forever before we pulled up in front of a rather large building that was situated at the top of a hill. There was long line of stone steps that appeared to be cut into the side of the hill, and led to what looked to be the front door.

The building had an ancient look to it. Almost as if the earth was made around it somehow. The walls were made of a deep shade of red brick that seemed to reach to the sky, and had an appearance of an ancient castle of sorts. I was ill impressed by the looks of our new home as well as the niceness from the older woman with us. I had a sickening feeling of what was in store for Tara and myself. Little did I know how right I was.

As we walked through the large double doors at the front of the building, the cathedral ceilings seemed to go up and on forever. I have to admit there was a sort of ancient beauty to this place. Directly across the room from the front doors stood a large statue of the Virgin Mary.

"Okay, girls." The old woman began. "All girls will sleep on the second floor. There will be no going to the third floor where the boy's dorms are." The orders seemed to cascade from the old woman's mouth as she continued. "There will be mandatory mass every day; as well as a list of chores that must be done each day. Am I understood?" The older woman spoke with renewed authority.

Yes, this place was no castle, nor would it conclude in a fairytale ending. I was hesitant to answer, but looked at my sister and nodded.

"Yes, ma'am." We both answered at the same time.

It was at that point that she led us up a curved staircase to the second floor. The halls were long and seemed as though they were never ending, but we finally came to an open door. Once inside, there were three rows of bunk beds. One row ran down the center of the room while the other two ran the length of the walls. I was almost glad to find an open bunk next to one of the windows, and had a feeling I would spend a fair amount of free time sitting there thinking about all that has recently happened.

I had no interest in making or keeping friends here, but decided to play nice when this fair skinned girl with deep red hair walked over to me.

"Hi. My name is Siobhan. What's yours?" She said.

"I'm Valentine and this is my sister Tara." I responded while pointing towards my sister.

"I won't keep you. I just wanted to introduce myself." She said. "Maybe we could be friends."

I didn't respond with words, but just nodded my head and forced a smile. Deep down I knew I wouldn't be here long, but how could I leave my sister right now? No, I would give her some time to adjust before hitting the road. I know deep down I would be breaking the last promise I made to my mother, but I had a new fire building within me. It was the fire of revenge and I had no desire to extinguish it.

The days seemed to drag by as my soul hardened. I wasn't at the orphanage long before I met a young man named Cian Callahan. He was a year older than me, had brown hair that seemed to flow on its own, and blue eyes that resembled the sky on a cloudless day.

Oh, my god! Was I falling in love with this guy? The answer was obvious, and it was yes. Yes, I was beginning to feel again. It was then that I decided it was time to leave. I had to keep my heart hard in order to learn how to get revenge for the murder of my parents.

On one of mine and Cian's afternoon walks I did the unthinkable. I had to make sure Tara would be taken care of.

"Cian, I have a question." I said

"Anything, Val." He responded while stopping to look me in the eyes.

"Please take care of Tara for me." My heart broke a little as the words formed in and then escaped my mouth.

"Val? What's going on? Why are you talking like this?" I could hear the fear in his voice as he realized he was about to lose me.

"Please just promise me that you will look after her for me! Cian, I need you to do this for me." I pleaded.

"I will, Val, but please don't do this. We can all leave together." He said as tears began to swell in his eyes.

"No! I need to know that Tara will be safe." I said as I turned away from him and ran.

I ran until it felt like my lungs would explode. I ran until I could no longer hear Cian calling out for me to stop.

CHAPTER
FOUR

My heart was in perpetual anguish for leaving my sister behind, but I knew she would be safe with Cian. I had to believe deep down that he would keep his promise to me and take care of her. I could only imagine the heartbreak and pain she was feeling now that I was gone. I just had to remind myself that this was for the best.

I walked until my legs fell out from under me, and landed face first into the ground next to a large tree. My vision blurred as I passed out from exhaustion. I woke up as the sun rose above the trees. My entire body was tired and sore from pushing it well past it's limits the night before. All I had were the clothes on my back, and somehow I believed that was all I needed.

"I've got to keep going." I encouraged myself, as I struggled to stand on two pain stricken wobbly legs. As I attempted to take a step, I stumbled, then collapsed onto the tree with my right shoulder making contact first. I stood there for a moment in an attempt to steady myself. For a quick painful moment, I thought I heard my mother's voice.

"Val, promise me you'll take care of your sister." She had said.

It was like a ghost haunting my deepest dreams. "I'm sorry mom." I said aloud as I began walking. I had to bury the memories of my parent's deaths and leaving my sister. My emotions needed to be in check.

I don't know how long I walked before coming to a small town. Fear that the orphanage would know now that I was missing set in, and a knot grew in my stomach at the thought that I would be caught. I found a small alleyway and decided to lay down to rest before moving on. I must have been more exhausted than I thought, because when I awoke I found myself laying in a bed. I had to regulate that fear and anxiety within me.

"Where am I?" I asked as if there were someone else in the room with me.

I had no idea where I was or what was in store for me, but somehow knew this was where I was supposed to be. My new life was beginning and I was flooded with emotions. Fear, anxiety, sorrow, and excitement all hit me at once.

It took a few minutes for me to learn how to move my arms and legs again. My entire body was heavy and sore from the journey I made over the last few days. My body hurt as I raised up to a sitting position in the bed and looked at myself in the mirror that was positioned directly in front of me next to the door. I hardly recognized the person staring back at me. My hair was disheveled and standing up everywhere. My face and clothes were a dirty mess from the dirt and mud.

I looked around the room. On the left side was a small dresser with a pair of black combat boots and what looked like military clothing folded on top. On the right side was a small sink and toilet. I forced my body out of the bed and sluggishly made my way over to the sink. I desperately needed to clean myself up.

There was a small towel rack next to the sink where I found a washcloth and bath towel. I grabbed the washcloth, wet it in the sink, and painfully made my way to the mirror by the door. I wiped my face until I could see a resemblance of myself again. I was amazed at the amount of dirt and grime that was stuck to the washcloth in my hands. I returned to the sink to rinse the cloth and began to wash away the dirt from the rest of my body.

Feeling somewhat clean, I made my way over to the dresser and picked up the first piece of clothing which was a solid black tank top. Having already taken my old dirty clothes off, I put it on. The next item was a pair of military style tactical pants, which surprised me when they fit perfectly. It was as if these clothes and this room were waiting for me my entire life. Had I finally found my place in this messed up world of mine?

I picked up the socks and military boots and walked over to the bed to sit down. It took me a few minutes to put the socks and boots on due to the extreme soreness in my body. I still had many questions floating in my mind. The most prominent one was how on earth did I get here, and where was here? I just sat there on the side of the bed and thought of the two most important people I left behind, and why.

It wasn't long before I heard a knock on the door, and a female voice.

"May I come in?" She said.

"Uh...yes." I answered back inquisitively.

I was a bit apprehensive as the door opened and a young woman entered. She was about average in height with short blond hair, and emerald green eyes. I felt like I fit in as she had on military clothing that resembled the clothes I was now wearing.

"I'm glad to see you are up and doing well. My name is Felicity. How are you feeling?" She asked.

"I'm okay. I'm just a little tired and sore." I said. "Where am I?"

"Don't worry about that now. Just know that you are safe here." She said. "What's your name sweetie?"

"Oh, uh...my name is Val." I replied.

It was at that point my stomach growled, and my hand instinctively covered it. I had forgotten that I hadn't eaten in quite a while. Felicity noticed the motion of my hand and stepped back outside the door. She returned with a tray of food and a silver cup. She walked over to where I was sitting and handed me the tray, but set the cup on top of the dresser.

"Here." She said. "You look like you could use this."

"Thank you." I said sheepishly.

She nodded and walked back to the door. Once there she turned back towards me and said, "Get some rest. I'll come back in the morning, and show you around a bit." She turned back towards the door and left closing the door behind her.

I had to remind myself to eat slowly, although I knew I was starving. It was some kind of carved meat, maybe turkey with potato mash and peas. There was also an end piece carved from a loaf of bread. I managed to nearly clean the tray only leaving a few slivers of meat and a couple stray peas that rolled around the tray as I got up to walk over to the dresser. I placed the tray on the dresser and picked up the metal cup. The contents looked like water, but had a strange fruity smell. After taking a small sip, I realized it had a grape taste.

They must have slipped something in the drink, because after a few gulps the room began to spin. I hardly made it back to the bed before passing out. The last thing I remember is hearing the metal cup make a ringing sound as it bounced on the floor when it fell from my hand.

The next thing I remember was hearing a knock at the door. Had I slept all night? I was ready for the soreness to hit as I moved to get out of the bed, but it was like I was a new person. My body felt refreshed and ready to go. "Come in!" I said, as I stood at the foot of the bed.

"Good morning, Val." Felicity said as she stepped just inside the door. "I trust you slept well, and you're ready for a long and eventful day."

"Yes ma'am." I said. "I'm feeling better today."

"That's good." Felicity said. "Come with me and I'll show you around a little. Then I'll show you where the mess hall is so you can eat. You'll then join your training group and start the day."

"Yes ma'am." I said with an eagerness to my voice.

We walked out of my room into a long hallway that seemed to go on forever in both directions. We made a right turn and began down the hallway. There were doors on both sides which I assumed were living quarters for the others in the training program. I still had the question in the back of my mind on how I got here in the first place, but didn't really seem to care anymore. This place felt like home to me now.

The first place we came to was a large room with punching bags, padded floor mats, and a variety of close combat weapons.

"This is the training room. You will come here to learn basic hand to hand combat." Felicity said as we stood in the doorway for a few moments more.

We continued walking through the catacombs of hallways until we came to another door. Housed there was what appeared to be an indoor shooting range. This room intimidated me a little as I had never picked up a gun in my life.

Felicity looked at me, smiled and said, "This is my favorite room. You will learn to hone your marksmanship here."

I had to agree with her that the room looked fun, and I was surprisingly looking forward to using a weapon for the first time. We visited several more rooms which had virtual fighting simulators, shooting simulators, and flight simulators. Was I supposed to learn how to fly something? The thought had my mind spinning. The last room we came to was the mess hall. Felicity looked at me with a kind but serious face and said.

"You will be with the blue team. The tables are marked accordingly. Find your table, make a few friends, and have a nice breakfast. Your training will begin soon."

She turned away from me and began to walk away. She took a few steps then turned around to look at me once more. "Oh yeah," she said. "Val, remember to have a little fun." She said with a wink, then turned and continued to walk away.

I walked into the mess hall knowing that the majority of the eyes in the room were on me. I made my way to the food line, which was set up in a buffet style, and picked up a plate. As I walked through the line I began to fill my plate. First with a helping of scrambled eggs, crispy bacon, hashed potatoes, and a piece of toast. Once my plate was full I made my way to the end of the line and picked up a carton of orange juice, then made my way to the blue team table. I could still feel eyes following me around the room. I know I'm the new person here, but this was beginning to irritate me.

While standing at the blue table I had every eye on me with an inquisitive look on each face. I decided to break the proverbial ice first.

"Hi. My name is Val." I said with a slight hint of nervousness in my voice.

"Hi Val. I'm Savanna. You can come sit here." She said. "This is Timothy." She added as she pointed at the young man sitting next to her.

I made my way over and sat down between them. I still had that hint of nervousness as I sat there and began eating. It was Savanna that spoke up first.

"Everyone, this is Val. She is new to our team." She said.

The next sound I heard was a hello and welcome Val in unison from everyone at the table. After that, everyone began eating again. I decided it was time to fill my stomach and prepare for what the day had in store for my team and I.

There was no time to "meet and greet" after we were all finished with breakfast. There was a voice that boomed over the intercom system.

"Blue team report to the combat room." It said.

CHAPTER
FIVE

I HAD NO IDEA WHAT WAS IN STORE as we started our warm up drills. We did a variety of push ups, sit ups, jumping jacks, and running in place for what seemed like hours. Then our instructor spoke up.

"Everyone to the mats. Let's have a little competition." He said.

We all moved to the mats that were set up in a square box like shape. My guess is it was supposed to be a form of boxing ring. I was hoping deep down that I wouldn't be chosen first for what was coming next. My hope was crushed as I heard our instructor once again.

"Okay. Max and Val. Center ring." He said as he looked me dead in the eye.

Great! I thought. I'm about to get the crap beat out of me. I hesitantly made my way to the center of the mat. I had no idea who Max was, and was surprised when a tall muscular guy stepped out of the crowd of blue team members.

Yep. I thought. This will be no fun at all. What in the hell was it going to prove, or even help me, to have the shit beat out of me? "Oh well." I said to myself. "Let's get this over with."

I raised my arms in a ready position to guard my face and body from an attack. Max did the same as the instructor gave the command to begin.

The first punch came as a surprise as Max's hand made contact with the right side of my face and knocked me back a little making me stumble on wobbly legs. Although I was a little rattled, I managed to duck away from his next punch and watched as his fist swung over my head. It was then that I heard Savanna.

"Come on, Val! You got this!" She yelled.

Her encouragement inspired me enough to land a punch to the left side of Max's face, then another punch contacted his chin as I used as much strength as possible to force each punch to make contact with Max. He took a couple steps back and shook his head. It must have angered him because he forced out an onslaught of punches and kicks that made contact to various areas of my body. His last punch hit its mark as I fell to the mat in a bruised and bloody heap. The instructor gave the nod for Max to finish the fight, and before I knew it everything went dark. I vaguely remember flashes of the instructor first checking my pulse, then lightly patting my cheek to ease me back to reality.

"You didn't do half bad, Val." He said. "But you have a lot to learn still. Savanna, Timothy, help Val up." He said as he walked away and began giving instructions to the others to begin their training.

As I sat off to the side of the room I could feel various parts of my face beginning to swell. I knew I would show the battle wounds of today's fight in the morning, and I would wear them with pride. Yes I lost the fight, but the biggest thing is I didn't give up. That in itself is a victory.

Over the next few months I became close friends with Savanna and Timothy. My strength and technique flourished along with my marksmanship. I went from being one of the questionable recruits to one of the best on my team. My hand to hand combat skills improved greatly and I was looking forward to my next encounter with Max. He may still beat me, but I'm sure that I could now give him a fair competition.

When it came to close combat weapons I decided to build my skills with knives and the escrima sticks. I was pretty dead on during all of our knife throwing lessons, always hitting center mass with each throw. This upset a small handful of my teammates as I started so low on the proverbial totem pole and was now one of the best.

My marksmanship improved as well. I started off missing the target more than I hit it. I spent the majority of my free time either in the combat room or in the range area training. I was adamant about becoming the best. I even tried my luck at the simulation rooms. They were more of a high tech virtual reality program than anything else. I do have to admit I loved being in there. It felt real which caused buried memories to arise and fuel my motivation.

"Val, you should come out with Timothy and I." Savanna said. "You deserve to give yourself a break and have a little fun."

"Thank you for the invite, Savanna, but I'm going to hit the range and then some VR time." I responded knowing deep down I wanted to go with them, and that I needed the break. I just couldn't lose my motivation with distractions. The thing is, Savanna never took no for an answer.

"No." She said. "Timothy and I and kidnapping you for a few hours. Then you can go back to being super assassin." She laughed after her last remark.

Did I really gain the reputation of being a super assassin? That's not exactly what I was going for, but hey, that's not a bad reputation to have. I wonder if everyone saw me that way? I had progressed quickly and shown intense dedication over the last few months.

"Okay, okay." I said as she grabbed my arm and dragged me off.

"Where are we going?" I asked.

"It's a surprise." Timothy responded with a hint of excitement in his voice.

Before I knew it I was being drug through the halls of our facility. We finally came to a set of stairs. That's when Savanna turned to me from a few steps up and said.

"Come on. It's just up here." She had a huge smile on her face.

Timothy was behind me lightly encouraging me to start up the steps. After a few flights of stairs I was beginning to wonder what my friends had in mind, and what their idea of fun was. We came to a door at the top of the stairs. I could only imagine that it led to the roof. My protective instincts began to kick in, but I pushed the thoughts and soon to be actions out of my head. These were my friends. The only friends I've had since...Cian. I thought as a feeling of regret and sadness welled up in me.

Savanna, being at the top of the stairs opened the door that led to the roof. She then turned and smiled at me. I couldn't help but wonder what they were both doing. Why the roof? Why tonight?

"Okay, close your eyes, and don't go all assassin on us." She said. "Timothy, help her up the steps please." She added.

I didn't like surprises, and the feeling was ever stronger now. But once I had firm footing on the rooftop, I had even more questions. I opened my eyes to see a setup under a homemade canopy. It looked like they set it up for a party. There was food on a table, and in the middle was a small cake. What was going on?

"We know you don't like surprises, but we figured you really needed this night. Happy birthday, Val." She said with a smile.

Had I told them about my birthday during our many conversations? I must have, and couldn't hold back the tear that trickled
down the side of my face. It was a tear from long buried memories. I was happy and sad all at the same time. Happy that my
friends had thought to do this for me, yet sad that my parents and
sister weren't here. I hated to feel! Things are much easier being a
hard ass, and I guess now a badass assassin.

"Thank you, guys." I said in a choked up voice. "This is really
amazing." I added as we walked over to the table and sat down.

We had a great time talking and laughing. Our conversations
were mostly about events at the facility. So much has happened
since I arrived here. This place really felt more like a home for
me rather than a place of intense training. I still had questions
on why so many young men and ladies were here learning how to
fight and kill. Little did I know I was soon to find out the answer
to that question.

I decided not to emerge myself in training that night. I went
to my room and looked at myself in the mirror for what seemed
like hours. Behind closed doors I decided to let it all out one final
time before letting it go forever. There was no better night than
the night of my birth. It was time to let go of who I was. I had
to let go of my parents, my sister, Cian, and most of all the girl
I once was. I know now I'm not that same little girl that arrived
here. Tomorrow was my challenge with Max, and there had to
be no more distractions. I knew I had to kill that little girl inside
and embrace the person I had become. It was then that I let the
tears flow.

I slept more soundly than I had in a very long time. I actually
don't remember dreaming. When I woke up I knew I was rested
and ready for my challenge today. If I can take Max today I will
be sent to the next level of training. I spent the majority of my

morning preparing myself for the afternoon's challenge, and by the time I reach the training room I felt secure and ready. I was going to take him this time. I just knew it.

Once our instructor called Max and I to the mat I decided to take my time walking up there. I guess I'm dramatic like that. I stood there looking Max in the eyes while waiting for the go ahead from the instructor. He seemed to have an inquisitive look on his face as I just stood there. I never bothered to get in the ready position as the instructor gave the go for our fight.

Max came at me fast and hard thinking he was catching me off guard. It was then that I laid and uppercut directly to his diaphragm knocking him off guard and sending him backwards heaved over from the unexpected blow. It was then that I charged him. I swung my leg in a crescent style kick and it connected with his head sending him in a heap on the mat. Max caught me a little off guard as he swung his legs knocking me to the mat next to him. He then jumped on top of me and tried to pin me down. I knew what was coming next and held my arms up to block his onslaught of punches towards my face and upper body. The first chance I got I wrapped my right arm round the left side of his neck, lifted my left hip, and managed to push him off of me. We spent several minutes grappling on the mat until I finally had Max pinned down and had his arm firmly placed in an armbar. It was then the instructor spoke up and proclaimed me the victor.

Finally! I thought. All of my dedication and training had paid off. I had successfully beat the largest and best fighter in our team. The instructor called me over to him.

"Well done, Val." He said. "Your moving on to the next stage of training, and don't think we haven't noticed all of the extra time you've been putting in." It was then that he gave me a half smile and walked away.

Savanna ran over to me ecstatic and clapping with Timothy in tow. The congratulations simmered as I told them I moving to the next level which mean a new team. Savanna's face grew dim so I spoke up.

"Don't worry. We will still see each other. This isn't goodbye." I said trying to reassure them. Or I should say reassure Savanna who seemed to take the news a lot harder. We knew our time spent together would be far and few between now. I had no thoughts on giving up on my friends. I know they would never do the same to me.

I soon found out what the next level of training was the next morning. I was now part of red team. We spent countless hours in the simulation room going through long range kills and close combat firearms kills. All of which I aced thanks to all of my previous training while on the blue team. It wasn't long before I moved up through the ranks of the team and became second in command. That had to change, because second place just doesn't do it for this girl. Or should I say woman now? I was now eighteen and at the final stages before moving on to active status. It had been a year and I rarely had any chances, due to training, to see Savanna and Timothy. The great thing was we never grew apart.

Savanna cried her eyes out when I mentioned my soon to be active status. Everyone knew what that meant. It would be rare occasions if ever that we would ever see each other again. I guess there was a reason to cry, but I just couldn't. I had no more emotion left within me. The three of us decided to plan another get together before I left. I looked down at my watch and realized it was time for my next "mission" so to speak. We were having war games with another team tonight and I was running a little late. I gave Savanna a hug and wiped the tears from her eyes.

"It will be okay, Savanna." I said as I jogged away.

This was a type of capture the flag game, and I wasn't exactly sure what to expect when I entered our red team meeting area. We had to wear high tech suits that would send low volt electrical pulses through the body when you were hit.

"This should be fun." I said to myself as I put on the suit. It fit rather tightly, but the electric probes were surprising unfelt.

"These look like loads of fun." James said as he looked at me while putting on his suit.

James was one of my squad leaders, and a good one at that. He was average in height and rather muscular. He usually spent the majority of his free time in the gym lifting weights. I had no doubt he would be a great asset to not only our team here, but to our team of actives. There were only a handful of us going active. Myself, James, and Max were among the chosen.

"James, call everyone to attention for orders." I said as I took my place next to the team captain Luke.

"Alright, team red! Everyone stand at attention and ready yourselves for your orders." James yelled with gusto and authority.

Our entire team came to attention with one loud clack of their boots on the floor. After that you could hear a pin drop as silence fell suddenly in the room. Every eye in the room was on our Luke and I. Luke spoke up first. I have to admit he had a certain amount authority to his voice that could strike fear into anyone.

"Listen up." He said. "The name of the game is capture the flag. I'm looking for as few casualties as possible tonight. I will lead a team to scout for the other team and their flag. Val will lead another team that will stand by until the signal is given to move in. Is everyone clear on your orders?"

The whole group spoke in unison, "Yes sir!" They responded.

"Good! Now, Val will have first choice of a team member."

Luke said.

"I'll take James." I said as James walked over to my side.

"I'll take Markus." Luke said. Markus was Luke's squad leader and was just as built as James.

Once we had our prospective teams we went over a map of the woods that are located outside of the facility. Once we knew where our positions would be Luke dismissed us and we set off. The officers, so to speak, had a type of handgun and a rifle to use. The others were given various types of riffles. I decided to obtain a long range sniper rifle in order to pick off the other team and give my team a chance to capture the other team's flag. I was however one of the best when it came to being a sniper. That was thanks once again to all of the training hours I put in during simulation.

Once in the woods I sent my team out and found a vantage point where I would have a clear view of the other team. They had pretty good defenses, but they were spread out too far.

"Easy pickings." I said to myself as I set up my rifle and waited for the signal from Luke.

It took a little while, but once Luke was in position and ready he gave me the signal which I noticed through my long-range scope. It was then that I gave James the go ahead, and began picking off the other team. I decided to hold a few of my team members back in order to guard an attack towards our flag. I did my best to keep my team members safe as they set toward the task of taking the opposing flag.

It wasn't long before I heard footsteps behind me. I laid in wait pretending that I didn't notice. I needed them to get a little closer in order to have a clear shot at them.

"I finally get to take out the big bad Val." I heard the voice behind me say.

Wait. I know that voice. It was Max, he was still a few hundred feet away but I slipped my hand down and drew my handgun from its holster and brought it up to chest level. After he took a few more steps I rolled over away from my rifle, held my side arm out and shot him twice in the chest. He then fell to the ground howling in agony as his suit sent out electrical pulses throughout his body. After I knew he was down I rolled back over to my rifle and continued my task of keeping my teammates safe.

I took out several of the other team's members all the while wondering in the back of my mind if the team recruited Max or if Savanna and Timothy were out there as well. The next person to come into focus in my scope was Savanna, and my question was answered. We were battling against the blue team. It killed me when I lined Savanna up in my crosshairs and began to squeeze the trigger.

"Sorry Savanna." I said as my rifle went off and she fell to the ground in pain.

It wasn't long before our team won the prize of the opposing team's flag. I could see one of Luke's group members swinging the flag in victory, and couldn't help but to smile. We only suffered a few casualties during the whole game. I don't know about Luke, but that was okay with me. The only regret I had was having to take Savanna down. No matter who's team she was on. It's never easy having to shoot a friend. Even if it was during a simulated war. I decided not to mention that I was the one to shoot her the next time I saw her, although I'm sure she knew already.

It didn't seem like a fair fight. The blue team was obviously not ready for the fight tonight. But then maybe tonight was about the red team. We were better organized and had a hand up on skill levels. I could hear the howls of victory as my teammates made their way towards me. Luke and I decided to have a small team meeting in the woods before heading back to the facility.

"Great job team." He began. "We only had a handful of us get hit which isn't bad." He went on. He looked over at me and said with a halfcocked smile, "Val, nice job." His final remarks were about the skill levels of some of the team members, then he dismissed us.

I decided to wait around a moment to see if I could catch up with Savanna. I could only guess that her team was having an impromptu meeting as well. I must have been right as I could soon see some of her team trickle through the woods. I could see Savanna at a distance. She looked up at me then quickly looked away. I knew then that she was upset about me shooting her. I decided to let her cool off and turned to make my way toward the facility and my room for a shower.

CHAPTER
SIX

I HAD NO SOONER GOTTEN OUT OF THE SHOWER and dressed when I heard a knock on my door. I inquisitively walked over and opened it. I wasn't sure if Savanna changed her mind about talking to me tonight, but had a surprise when I saw who was standing there. It was Felicity. I hadn't talked with her in a very long time.

"Hi, Val." She said. "May I come in?"

"Sure." I responded as I moved over to allow her access to my room.

I know she could see the questions in my eyes and on my face. Why was Felicity showing up now of all times? I hated surprises, and more than that I hated not knowing what was going on. I'm the type of person that wants to be well informed.

"I know you're wondering why I'm here." She began. "As you know you will be going active soon. You have made quite a name for yourself behind these walls, Val." She went on. "You have grown so much since you've been here with us and have become quite strong in every aspect."

"Thank you, Felicity." I responded. "I have been keeping myself focused on the task at hand all this time."

"That focus will come in handy soon. As you may already know you're one of the few chosen to go into active status. You will need to keep focused and vigilant with everything you do and every move you make. It won't be like it is here." She said. "It's the real thing out there, and people will not hesitate to kill you."

I had no response to her last remark and just shook my head in agreement. I hadn't imagined in my wildest dreams that I would become an assassin, and it seemed that this road chose me.

"Well, I'll let you get some rest. I'm sure you have an early morning of training. Have a good night, Val." She said as she walked out and shut the door behind her.

After Felicity left I stood and took a long look at myself in the mirror. I can honestly say I didn't recognize the reflection. I wasn't the same person that arrived here so long ago. I took another few minutes to take in the image staring back at me then walked over to my bed and heavily fell onto it. It had been one hell of a day, and night for that matter.

I laid there thinking about what Felicity told me about being on the outside. I knew deep down I was ready for becoming an active assassin, I just hated the fact that I would be leaving behind Savanna and Timothy. The three of us had grown so close over the last couple of years. The thing I hated most was not knowing whether or not I would ever see or hear from them again after I left.

I woke up early the next morning and headed to the simulation room to get in a little training before breakfast. After a few hours of killing virtual bad guys I decided to break the rules a little during breakfast. I grabbed my tray and made my way over to the blue team's table. I could see Savanna and Timothy sitting next to each other clearly in deep conversation. I walked up behind them, and while holding my tray with one hand tapped Savanna on the shoulder. She turned and looked at me in surprise.

"Can I squeeze in?" I asked.

I could see the questions in her's and Timothy's eyes as they looked up at me from the table. I knew they were wondering why I was requesting to sit at their table instead of with my own team.

"Uh...sure." Savanna responded while giving Timothy an inquisitive glance.

"Thanks." I replied as I sat my tray down and squeezed between the two of them at the table. "Are we still on for tonight?" I asked once seated.

"Umm...YES!" Savanna said enthusiastically.

I have to admit that made me feel better. I still had a feeling she was harboring some hard feelings about me shooting her the night before.

"Oh, by the way, Val. Thanks for shooting me last night." She said with a wink.

"Yeah, sorry about that. I got wrapped up in the game." I laughed in retort.

It was then that I saw Max giving me an malevolent look from further down on the other side of the table. I couldn't help but to give him a sinister smirk in response. I could see that that only fueled his anger about me besting him both on the matts and in the field. Although we didn't really like each other, we has a sort of respect for one another.

"Yeah," Savanna started. "I can't say it didn't hurt on a couple levels." She laughed.

"I knew you were a little upset last night and figured I'd let you cool off. I just wanted to make sure there was no bad blood between us." I said.

"Of course not, Val. You're my best friend."

"Hey! What am I? Chopped liver?" Timothy chimed in.

Savanna and I both looked at each other and then turned to Timothy and laughed.

"No, not chopped liver. Maybe a little lamb chop though." I

said with a smile.

Timothy said nothing but smiled in response. I was truly going to miss these two when I leave. We sat and ate while having idle conversation about things we were going through and things to come. Before we knew it, time had flown by and it was time for us to go our separate ways for the day's training. I was surprisingly excited about and looking forward to sharing some free time with Timothy and Savanna.

My training day was light with a little hand to hand combat training, weapons training, and firearms training. Luke and I both agreed that last night's victory warranted a light and early day, which was approved by our instructor.

I decided to spend most of the afternoon in my room with nothing but my thoughts. I had so many things swimming through my mind. I was thinking about my friends and wondering what warnings if any I would share with them tonight. I also had thoughts about Cian and Tara. I tried to envision what they might be doing at this very moment, and where they were. I'm sure that by now Cian would've taken Tara away from the orphanage, and hoped he would keep his promise to take care of her for me. I decided to hold on to the hope that I would one day see them both again someday. I had a deep suspicion that hope would carry me through the toughest of times to come.

I still didn't like the feeling of not know exactly what I was about to get myself into once I leave here. My past has shown me that this world can be an extremely harsh place. I would have to just be much worse than this world

I must have lost myself in my thoughts because the next thing I knew there was a knock at the door, then Savanna's voice calling through it.

"Val! Val, are you in there?" She asked.

"Uh...yeah!" I called back. "Come in, Savanna."

She slowly opened the door and looked in my direction. I'm sure she could see that I had been in deep thought. I could feel that my eyebrows were still a little furloughed indicating the latter.

"Everything okay?" She asked.

"Yeah. Just thinking about some things." I replied as I rubbed my forehead in order to relax the already tense muscles. I had decided to keep my past a secret since the day of my arrival here. No one needed to know about my parents or my sister. I didn't relish the fact that I was keeping things from Savanna, but I truly believed it was better this way.

"If you say so, Val. I've learned not to push you with questions. So, are you ready to go?" She responded clearly concerned with my recent behavior and silence towards certain questions.

"Yes. Is it time already?" I said as I grabbed my jacket and walked over to where Savanna was standing by my door.

Savanna put her arm around my neck and said, "Val, I don't know what's going on, but I'm sure that whatever it is, you can handle it. You are the strongest person I know."

I looked at her and gave a half smile which was all I could muster at the moment. My mind was still swimming with thoughts, and it was a little too soon to pretend that everything was fine. We were close enough that she knew I had some things going on, but she didn't push me for answers and I loved her for that. We continued down the hall with our arms around each other's shoulders and I took some comfort from that.

"Is Timothy waiting for us on the roof?" I asked once we arrived at the base of the stairs. I had no reason to suspect a surprise tonight since we planned this get together weeks ago.

I let Savanna start up the stairs ahead of me and continued my attempt to control the thoughts swimming in my head. I wanted this night to be fun for all three of us, and didn't want my inner demons to ruin it. I was weary about divulging my personal information to anyone. Even those closest to me. Once we got to the roof Timothy was sitting on a pillow waiting under our homemade canopy.

"Good. No surprises tonight." I thought to myself as Savanna and I walked over to where Timothy was sitting. "Hey there lamb chop." I said jokingly to Timothy as I sat down on one of the pillows.

"Are you seriously going to keep calling me that?" He asked.

"Why not? It's better than chopped liver, right?" I said with a smile.

"Not funny." He retorted with a smile. "So what's been going on with you lately? Still spending all your time in the simulation room with your sniper rifle?"

"You know it." I said. I have to admit. My friends knew be better than I thought. "What about you guys? How's the training going?"

"Well, Max still has some hard feelings towards you for shooting him." Timothy said.

"As do I." Savanna chimed in with a smile. "I'm just glad you're ultimately on our side, Val. You're one hell of a shot."

We both looked at Timothy who nodded in agreement. It was such a nice clear night. The air was a little cool which every once in a while, gave me a chill. Each time I felt a shiver from the light breeze I was glad I decided to take my jacket along. The three of us just sat and talked and laughed while looking at the stars, which could clearly be seen. It wasn't often that the sky would be so clear. It was almost as if there wasn't a cloud in the sky. Usually the sky would be mostly cloudy, and a mist could be felt in the air. Tonight was different, and it was a welcomed change.

"Look Val." Savanna said as she tapped my shoulder and pointed towards the sky. "There's your lucky star."

It was at that point I looked up and saw a shooting star streak across the sky in front of us. Deep down I hoped she was right about the luck. I'm sure I was going to need it sooner than later.

"Doesn't the luck go to the first person to see it?" I asked.

"I think Val's right, Savanna." Timothy said.

"Nah. I give the luck to you, Val. You might need it." She replied.

"You guys really are the best." I said. "And thank you, Savanna, for the luck." I said as I turned and smiled at her while leaning over to nudge her shoulder with mine.

Timothy looked at me with a serious look and asked, "have you heard anything about when you might be leaving?"

"No, but I'm sure it won't be long from now. I had a visit from Felicity last night." I replied knowing I shouldn't say too much about the talk she and I had.

"Really? Felicity came to see you?" Savanna asked now show signs of concern on her face.

"Yeah. She was just telling me what a good job I was doing, and saying how much I had grown since being here." I said trying to ease Savanna's worries. She had a habit of worrying too much, and I feared that would be a huge weakness for her.

"So, do you have any advice for us before you leave?" Timothy asked.

"Well, as a matter of fact I do." I started. "Stay focused on your training." I stopped and just sat there for a moment.

"Oh, is that all." Savanna said with a smirk.

I laughed at her sarcasm. "No that's not all." I said. "Remember to be there for each other. We will always be a team." I said as I began to feel that familiar heartache as the words came out of my mouth. Was I losing yet another family? Timothy and Savanna must have seen the change of expression on my face to one of a familiar pain.

"Val? Are you okay?" Timothy asked.

"Yeah. I'm good." I said while trying to compose myself. "I'm just going to miss you both is all."

"We feel the same way, Val." Savanna said as she began to tear up once again. I have to admit I was concerned about her future and hoped she would only have to perform surveillance jobs instead of possibly have to kill someone. It seemed she didn't have the right mindset for the things we were being trained to do, and decided to wait until we were alone to talk to her about that.

We sat on the roof for a while longer. Neither of us said much after Savanna's emotional waiver. We just sat in silence enjoying each other's company, and the beautiful night sky. After a while we each agreed it was time to call it a night and headed back inside. Once we reach the bottom of the stairs we, said our goodnights. It was then that I hooked my arm around Savanna's in order to hold her back a moment while Timothy disappeared down the hallway.

"Savanna." I began. "I do have one vital piece of advice for you."

She looked at me and her face had a clear look of curiosity as she waited for me to continue. "Val, what's going on?" She couldn't help but ask before I had a chance to say anything further.

"I guess I could say this is more of a request from me. I don't want to see anything bad happen to you, and things are only going to get tougher as time goes on. Not just here, but when you get out as well." I began. I was attempting to lighten the blow in case she may take my next few words the wrong way. "I need you to toughen up. You need to try to bury the emotions that easily overcome you. They will only serve to be your enemy."

I could see she was processing what I just said, so I continued. "You mean a lot to me, and I don't want to see or hear of anything bad happening to you." That last comment seemed to sink in further, and I could tell she was understanding my point.

"Thank you, Val. I know you're right. I am a little soft and pretty open when it comes to my emotions." She said, then looked down at the floor. "Can I ask how you have been able to do that? I mean, I know you must have been through so much before coming here, and there are times that I can see some emotions arise in you. It's just you have so much control that at those moments you seem to keep yourself in check."

I wasn't sure what to tell her, so I just opened up to her on what I had to do in order to bury my life deep within. "Savanna," I began. "The secret to my self-control was standing in front of my mirror staring at myself, and realizing that I needed to let whatever happened in my past and whoever was left there go." I said.

She looked at me and I could see that she didn't quite understand what I had just told her. I knew this conversation was going to take a little longer and requested that she return with me to my room in order to let her in on my past. I still had my reservations about opening up to anyone, but I felt I could truly trust Savanna.

Once in my room, I looked at Savanna and began my story. Before I started I had to make her promise to keep everything I said to herself. I told her frist about my parents. "Savanna, I watched both of my parents die. I actually held my mother in my arms as she took her last breath." I said as she slowly began to understand my motivations. "My sister and I were taken to an orphanage where I spent most of my time. It was there that I met Cian. He and I were extremely close to one another. I made him promise me that he would take care of my sister just before I ran away."

She looked at me with an expression of concern and empathy.

"Val, I'm so sorry. I have no idea what to say about this." She said. "How do you keep all of that buried inside? I mean, how can you not let all of that affect you?" She asked.

I looked at her with all seriousness and said, "Savanna, that's my motivation here." I knew she then understood what I was saying, and knew what point I was trying to make.

She looked at me with a look of understanding on her face. "Thank you, Val." she said as he put her arms around my neck and hugged me tight and long.

We spent a little more time just enjoying and taking comfort from each other's company. I felt a sense of relief after divulging my deepest past to Savanna. It was almost like a huge weight had been lifted off of me. I knew and had a deep hope that I could trust Savanna to keep what I told her to herself.

Before she left for the night we gave each other on last hug. She walked over to the door seeming to be in deep thought about the things I told her. Once she got to the door and put her hand on the knob, she turned and looked at me, "no worries, Val. This will stay between you and me." She said as she opened the door and walk out.

I knew this would be the last time I would see them. I decided to write them both a letter.

Savanna, just remember what I told you. If you can do what I asked, everything will be okay.

I'm going to miss you so very much. Please try to find me once you get out. You are the first and closest friend I have found since being here. I'm not going to lie, things are going to get tougher as time goes on. You can do this! You are so much stronger than you think you are.

With much love and respect, Val

I folded the letter and put her name on the outside of it, then wrote one for Timothy.

Timothy, please keep an eye on and watch over Savanna. She has a strong spirit but a soft heart. I know you two are going to be great, and will be okay once I'm gone. I've asked her to find me once she is out. I'm going to ask the same of you. You both are like family to me, and I want you to be strong and safe. I hope to see you again soon.

With much love and respect, Val

I did the same with the letter to Timothy, and left them on the small table under my mirror. I knew they would be delivered to them both once I was gone. I knew I wouldn't get the chance to say a proper goodbye, and hated that. At least they would have a small piece of me with the letters.

It wasn't long after I finished writing the letters and putting them on the table that Felicity tapped on my door, then opened it without warning or an invitation.

"Val." She said. "It's time to go. quickly pack your things and come with me."

I did as she said knowing I had no other choice. All of my choices were now stripped from me, and I now had orders to follow.

CHAPTER
SEVEN

IT HAD ONLY BEEN A FEW MONTHS since my departure from the training facility, and all of my orders, or missions, had been the surveillance of potential targets and of others like myself. The organization frowned upon their soldiers, or assassins to leave the organization.

I traveled to so many places around the world that I often lost track of where I was or where I was going. The organization kept me so busy and on the go so much that I had no time to think. Maybe that was the point. Maybe that was their way of making me forget everything but the mission. I have to say that it was working. I hadn't thought about my family, Timothy, or Savanna in so long that they were slowly being wiped from my memory.

I know it's only been a few months, but I was starting to get the itch to shoot someone or something. Maybe I'll find a shooting range and sharpen my skills if I ever get some down time. Just as I had that thought my phone went off. I looked down and noticed I had a text message from my contact at the organization.

You have a few days of down time. Take this time to rest before your next mission.

"Finally." I said to myself as I read the text. I decided to take a flight back to my home land. I missed Ireland so much and felt that a few days there would help me more than taking rest at one of our safe houses. I knew the dangers of what I was planning to do, but I knew in my heart it had to be done. I had made up my mind. I'm going home, dangerous or not.

I took my time on my flight from Italy to Ireland to think of those I've left behind. My first thought went to Cian and Tara. I couldn't help but wonder where they were and what they were doing. Were they living their lives, or were they on a mission to find me? I had to make sure I was far enough away that they wouldn't find me. I wasn't ready to go back to them and believed I would put them in danger. I didn't want the organization to know about them, and knew they were better off without me for that very reason.

My mind swam with thoughts of Savanna and Timothy as I sat there looking out of the widow of the plane. All I could see was the ocean, so I closed my eyes for a moment and thought back to our meetings on the roof of the facility. I wondered if they were still in the facility, or if they were finally out and active. I began to feel that familiar feeling for sadness and loss, and took a moment to compose myself before letting my thoughts continue.

I wished I knew how to get in touch with Savanna or Timothy. I hoped they received my letters and would try to find me once they were out. It would be nice to see at least one familiar face, and soon.

I still worried about Savanna. She has such a tender heart, but an extremely strong spirit. I fear her softness and tender heart would be her downfall. If she was out, I feared for her, but hoped she took our last talk seriously and did as I asked of her. Savanna had become like a sister to me during our training, and I loved her as such. I would die to protect her, and knew she would do the same for me.

I spent the next hour or so of the flight looking out of the window and just let my mind go to whatever thoughts it wanted to. I guess you could say I just daydreamed about the past and the future on and off. That seemed to make the time fly by as the next thing I knew the flight attendants announced we were beginning our descent into Ireland.

I couldn't help the feeling of excitement that began to build up inside of me as the plane landed and we couriered to our prospective gate at the airport.

"Finally home." I said to myself as I got out of my seat and grabbed my overnight bag from the overhead compartment. As the plane was making its stop at the gate I made my way to the door of the plane. I really hate to fly, and the faster I get off this plane the better.

After making off the plane, in record time I might add, I quickly made my way through the small airport to where the rental car stations were located. I had no need to go to the luggage area, because everything I owned was in one small bag that was securely hung across my neck and shoulders.

After reaching one of the rental stations I rented a small car and began my drive out to the country. I felt I needed to be in somewhat of a secluded area, so I drove until I was at least a few towns away from the airport. I knew that any gun range I went to would not compare to the range I used while in the facility, but I needed that release. Not to mention the smell of freshly burnt gunpowder was something I was craving right now.

I decided to stay at a small rundown hotel just outside of town. I knew deep down that I was never off the radar of the organization. I was sure they knew exactly where I was, and more than likely knew my plans. At this point I didn't care. Just being back home in Ireland was giving me the motivation I desperately needed right now.

Once inside my small room at the motel, I sat down in front of the mirror and looked at the shell of the person that reflected back at me. I took the time to think of my parents. The memories haunted me, and each time I allowed them to come up it felt like it was only yesterday that I watched them die. I let the memory of holding my mother as she took her last breath linger just long enough to ignite furry inside of me. As much as I hated any emotion, I needed them. I especially needed the emotions that would keep me on task. Furry was one of those emotions that did the job.

I lingered in front of the mirror for a little while longer before getting up and going into the tiny bathroom to take a shower. I desperately needed to wash the day away. There's nothing like a day of traveling to make you feel exhausted and dirty.

Once showered and feeling a bit more at ease, I made my way to the full-sized bed and heavily fell onto it. I laid there and took some time to clear every thought from my mind before falling asleep.

I awoke the next morning to the sound of a door closing. Maybe a car door outside? Either way, it was time to start my day. I quickly got dressed and made my way to the closest gun shop I could find. This was no hard task given the city I chose to stay in.

It was a small shop, but had everything I was looking for. I bought a long range rifle and a .45 handgun along with ammo for both. The shop owner gave me an inquisitive look as I made my purchase, but I paid no attention. I thanked him and left with a small smile on my face.

The next task was to find a range to use my new toys. That again was no hard task as there was an indoor range not far from the gun shop. I pulled up to the large building and had a feeling they would have what I needed. I spent a little while firing my handgun and sharpening my aim since it was a little off after not having fired a weapon in so long. Once I felt comfortable with the handgun, I moved to the area of the range for rifles. I hoped my aim would be a little better there since I bought one of the best scopes on the market. It took me a few shots to get the sights lined up, but then I was hitting dead on.

I was right that the smell of freshly burnt gunpowder would lift my spirits. I left the range once all of the ammo I purchased was spent, and had a feeling of utopia as I got back into my small rental car. Yes, my day was well spent, and I now had the firearms I would soon need.

It was starting to get late in the day, and realizing that I hadn't eaten, I stopped on my way back to the hotel and grabbed some takeout. I was in no way tired as I got back to my room, so I ate then cleaned my weapons. One of the most important lessons I learned during my training was not only to protect yourself, but to always keep your weapons clean.

I spent a few hours that night taking apart and putting my guns back together. This served as an outlet to keep my mind occupied on something other than my thoughts and emotions. I had enough of those last night.

I took a look over at the small alarm clock on the nightstand and noticed it was after midnight. I knew I would have yet another message from the organization the next day and figured I should get some rest. My sleep was restless during the night. I had dreams of the day I ran away from the orphanage, Cian, and Tara.

I awoke the next morning to the phone ringing. I slowly picked up the receiver and answered. "Hello."

"Val?" The voice on the other end said.

No. The voice sounded scarcely familiar to me. It can't be. It was Tara! How the hell did she find me?

"I'm sorry. You have the wrong number." I said trying to dismiss her.

"'Val. Please don't hang up. It's me. Please!" she said.

"I'm sorry." I said again. "You have the wrong number." It was then that I hung up the phone and quickly packed my things.

"I have to get out of here." I said to myself as I threw my things in my car.

Once on the road I realized what a mistake it was coming back here. I knew they would be looking for me. I couldn't let them get close to me right now. It wasn't safe for them around me, and keeping myself as far away as possible was for the best. I knew now that I could never come back home.

It wasn't long while on the road that I received the message I was waiting for. My pager went off with yet another message, and I'm sure another mission. I guess it was a good thing I was already making my way back to the airport.

I waited and drove a little while before pulling over to read the message. I was a bit surprised at what I read.

You are to go to South America. There you must find one Mr. Victor Santana. Your mission is to find and neutralize your target.

"South America it is." I said to myself as I sped off spinning the tires of my small car and made my way toward the airport. I have to admit, I was nervous and excited about this mission.

Once back at the airport I first returned my car to the rental station, then made my way to the ticket counter where I purchased my ticket to South America. I checked my weapons at the counter since I obviously couldn't take them on the plane. I had to upgrade my ticket to first class in order to catch the first flight out. This is where the perks of having a credit card with no limit came in quite handy. Only this card was traced by the organization. Once I use it, they can track me anywhere.

Once my checked baggage was on its way to the plane, I made my way through the security check area. This was the one thing, other than flying, that I hated. Luckily the airport was sparsely filled with people, and the lines at the security check area were small. I still had a little time before my flight out, so I took my time walking to the gate.

It worked because one at the gate they were already starting to board the plane. Being a first class passenger I was one of the first people on the plane. I put my small overnight bag in the overhead compartment and took my seat which was once again by the window.

Once the plane was loaded and making its way down the runway, I put in my headphones. This was not only to occupy my mind, but to serve as a warning that I didn't want to be disturbed during the flight. I knew once I landed at the connecting airport I would need to find somewhere to have my hair cut. This was a sad but necessary task. I loved my long red hair and dreaded the thought of having it all cut off.

The first connecting airport was in London. "I'm sure I can find a place there." I thought to myself while in flight. It wasn't long before we were descending into London, and finally getting off the plane. I quickly made my way to the closes beauty shop, if you could call it that. I made the decision to get a very short hair style.

"This should serve to be functional." I said to myself after thanking the stylist and paying her. I left the shop and found a small vender to get something to eat. I had a little time before my connecting flight and I spent it deep in thought about my upcoming mission. I had to come up with some kind of game plan.

How was I going to find Victor? Most importantly, how was I going to ensure my safety. There was no way I was going to die on my first assassination mission. I know I've been keeping myself up with my hand to hand combat skills and making sure I stayed healthy and strong, but I still had no idea what I was getting myself into. Surveillance was going to be the key to my survival on this mission. I needed to take time to know who and what I was dealing with.

Before I knew it, I heard the boarding call for my connecting flight, and made my way to the gate. I had only one more connection before reaching South America. I was flying into Rio de Janeiro, and was glad that Portuguese was one of the many languages I decided to learn.

I was once again next to the window, which I despised. I guess it was the vulnerability of sitting next to a window and not knowing what was out there. The next flight was the same. Yet another window seat. I had the same routine for each flight. I put my headphones in, once in flight, to limit any form of interruptions to better prepare for this new mission.

It was a couple of hours before we landed in Rio, and my first task once I gathered my belongings from the the plane, then my bags from the baggage claim area. Those were the most important ones. My first task was to change my hair color, so I needed to find a salon away from the airport. This was due to the fact that I no longer wanted to be around a horde of travelers in the airport.

Once out and about in Rio, I found a slinky hotel to stay in for a while. After settling in, I walked around and found a salon and walked in, and asked to have my hair color changed. I decided to go with blond with a small amount of pink in my bang area.

"Posso ajudá-lo, mam?" One of the ladies asked. Which in English was, how may I help you.

I decided to use the native tongue and asked for the change in hair color. "Eu gostaria de mudar minha cor de cabelo. Isso é possível fazer agora?"

"Sim, senhora." She replied. Meaning yes ma'am.

It wasn't long before I was sitting in a chair and having my hair color changed. Thank god! This was a much needed change. I couldn't risk being noticed or recognized by anyone. This wasn't my first time in Rio.

After doing all of the necessary changes, I decided it was time to begin my work and find out as much as I could about my new friend Victor. I made my way to my room at the motel and began working. It wasn't long before I found out all the dirty secrets he was trying to hide. Once I reported back to the organization the intell I gathered, it was time to start the job of looking for and neutralizing my target.

CHAPTER
EIGHT

I MUST HAVE LOST TRACK OF TIME, which could be mostly due to the copious amounts of alcohol I drank to drown my memories and emotions. I woke up to the sound of the alarm on my phone going off. It was time for the summit meeting downstairs. I got up feeling a little tipsy still and decided to go to the restroom to wash my face in some cold water in an attempt to sober myself.

The cold water didn't quite do the job as I was still having trouble walking and thinking straight. What the hell was I thinking drinking so much? I know I wanted to drown the emotions that began to bubble up while talking to my target. He seemed oddly familiar to me, but I just couldn't put my finger on it.

It seemed like I knew him from somewhere. His face was very familiar to me. Maybe I should do a little more research on him. I want to know everything before having to neutralize him. That was my plan to begin with, but I have a feeling there's more to his story. My research will have to wait though until after the meeting.

I was undercover as a Russian diplomat, and had to make an appearance at this meeting. This was the opening meeting of several to come this week. I plan to watch his every move at this meeting. You can learn a lot about someone just by the way they act around other people. Let's see what I can learn tonight about Mr. Maseru.

I took a little time to clean myself up before heading down the hall to the elevators. I was thankful that I didn't run into Tripp while waiting for the elevator. A one on one confrontation with him was not what I wanted right now. The chat with him earlier was enough for one day. There was something about him that brought up old memories and feelings that I had long forgotten. I need to stay focused on what needed to be done right now, and can't deal with or need any form of distractions.

The elevator ride down to the main floor seemed like a long one, and I was somewhat grateful for that. I was alone on the ride down, which aided in building my composure. I'm still angry and disappointed in myself for drinking so much. Especially knowing I had so much work that needed to be done still.

Before reaching the ground floor, I looked at my reflection in the mirrors at the back of the elevator to make sure I was present-able for this meeting. My plan was clear. I was going to find a seat in the rear in order to observe not only my target, but all those there for this long week of summit meetings. These meetings were meant to warrant peace in the area, and none other than Tripp was one of the main players here.

Once the elevator doors opened, I hastily made my way to the bar inside of the hotel. I ordered a drink, mostly for show, since I had clearly had enough earlier in the day. I sat for a while and sipped my glass of cherie while vigilantly watching each person that made their way into the suite where the conference meetings were being held.

It wasn't long before Tripp made his way through the doors, but he wasn't alone. He had a young woman walking arm and arm with him. She was beautiful in her own right with long blond hair that laid out with full bouncy curls at the ends. She was slen-der, and short in size, but wore a magnificent long black dress with beauty and grace.

My orders were clear in obtaining as much information about Tripp as possible then kill him. My orders said nothing about the young woman in his tow. This site made my decision to gather more intel on Tripp all the more important. I may seem like it by my actions, but I'm no monster. I will not take an innocent life no matter the company they choose to keep. I felt the need to find out who this woman was as well, and report it back to the organization. I may end up with two targets on this mission depending on what information I can dig up on both of them.

My task now was clear. I would need to introduce myself to her once this meeting was concluded. Having a clear plan in place I made my move and made my way into the hoard of people that were in attendance for the meeting. My timing was perfect as the only available seating was near the rear of the large room. It seemed that there were rows of chairs as far as the eye could see. Each chair was occupied from the front of the room to the rear. There was a large platform that was perfectly placed in the center at the front of the room, and harbored a large table with multiple microphones that seemed evenly place along its length.

The meeting was long, and I must say extremely boring. I paid little attention to the ramblings coming from the front of the room. All of my focus was on my now two targets. After watching them for a while it seemed they met more new acquaintances than people they already knew for a man of his title. Something seemed off about that.

Who were these two people? It almost seemed as though they were working undercover as well. If that were the case, I had two questions. Who are they, and who do they work for? Their actions in the crowd confirmed my suspicions, and only fueled my desire to uncover the truth they were trying so hard to hide. All of the questions and concerns I had about Tripp and his female companion flooded my mind as I made my way through the crowd to where they were standing. I would need to get close to them in order to attempt my plans to gain more knowledge about, and find out who they were.

I walked slowly towards them in an attempt to time my introduction just after the couple they were already talking to walked away. As I walked up, Tripp's lady friend was the first to turn in my direction then smiled. She had a beautiful smile that seemed to light up the room.

"Hi, I'm Jessica." She said while extending her hand in my direction.

"Hello, Jessica." I said taking her hand in mine and giving it a slight shake. "My name is Svetlana. "I haven't seen you at any of the previous summits before. What did you think of the first meeting?"

"It was quite interesting. Although, I must say I did get a bit bored near the middle. Are all the meetings like the one tonight?" She asked.

I gave her a smile at her honesty and replied, "No." I said. "Some of them are much more mundane, and only get worse as the week progresses."

She gave a half frown while her eyes drifted down towards the floor. "How can you stand to sit through them?" She asked without looking up.

I gave a slight giggle at her question. The truth was, I had never been to a summit for peace, much less this particular one. How was I going to get this young lady to open up and talk with me? I suddenly had a brilliant idea, and asked, "hey, would you like to come and have a couple drinks with me sometime this week?" This was a great plan if she decided to take the bait. "We could use it as excuse to get out of a few of these ever boresome meetings."

She looked up at me with a slight grin on her face. "That would be great." She said.

"It's done then." I said with a smile. "Meet me at the bar around noon tomorrow."

"Sounds like a plan." She responded as we shook hands and said our goodbyes for the evening.

With my plan set in place I made my way back to the elevators. I had no interest in the meeting that was still going on. I knew I was taking a risk in blowing my cover by doing this, but I was in no shape to sit through that meeting after all I drank earlier. I still can't believe I let myself lose control like that. This was yet another sign that it was time to retire and leave all of this behind.

There were only a few people waiting for the elevators, and luckily Tripp was not one of them. I didn't need another confrontation with him. Not yet at least. Once the elevator doors opened each of us walked in and pressed the buttons on the wall for our prospective floors, and the doors closed. It seemed to take forever to reach my floor as the elevator stopped at every other floor to let the others off. I was one of the last people left on the elevator. There was a young man who must have been in his early thirties on the elevator with me.

Not trusting anyone, I took a defensive stance at the back of the elevator and waited for the doors to open on my floor. He was a handsome fellow with longer dark brown hair and crystal blue eyes. He just stood there for a few moments looking at me, then spoke.

"Do I know you from somewhere?" He asked.

I was reluctant to answer but did anyways. "No. I'm not from around here. I'm just here as an assistant for the meetings this week." I replied. "I must have a what do you call it, familiar face."

I added.

"Maybe that's it." He said with a wink. "If I'm not being too bold, it is a beautiful face."

"That is a bit bold, but thank you." I replied as the doors opened on my floor. "Have a good night." I added as I walked off the elevator not giving him a second look. I have only one true love in my life, and I painfully left him a long time ago. Perhaps I would see him and my sister again after this last job.

"You have a good night as well, beautiful." He called after me as the elevator doors were closing.

I slowly walked to my room. I had so much swimming through my mind. The first and foremost thought was how I was going to get the information I needed about Tripp. The second was the gentleman in the elevator did look a bit familiar to me, but where could I possible know him from?

Once in my room I sat at the small desk and began my work. I pulled my computer out of the bag and opened it to begin searching the internet for any information I could find on Tripp. I couldn't get the man from the elevator out of my mind. The more I thought about it the more I believed I knew him. I decided to search my memory for him. It didn't take long before I realized who he was. It was James. What the hell was he doing here?

Fear set in for a moment. Had the organization found out my plans to leave? Had they sent James to make sure I completed the job, or was he sent to take care of me for planning to leave the organization. I knew I was under strict supervision being one of their best assassins, but how did they find out? I hadn't mentioned my plans to anyone but myself. In light of this discovery, I couldn't let this distract me from the job that needed to be completed. My focus needed to be on taking out Tripp, then I can focus on James and the organization.

My plan, if all went well, was to ignore the fact that I knew James was here. I had to convincingly pretend that I hadn't recognized James in the elevator, and hope that he would believe it. For now, it was time to get back to work trying find any information I could about Tripp and his female companion, Jessica. Exhaustion got the better of me as I dozed off a few times while sitting at the computer. Having little success finding any information through various search engines, I made my way to the bed to get a little rest.

I must have been extremely exhausted because I don't remember dreaming the night before. It has been an extremely long time since I've slept that deeply, and it worried me that I was able to now. There was too much going on for me to be this calm and, for a lack of a better word, out of it. I need to finish this mission so I can get the hell out of dodge, and get lost in all literal senses of the word.

I spent the better part of the morning trying to search for any information on Tripp and Jessica. I don't remember a time when I had to work so hard to research a target. All of my attempts to find information on both of them were unsuccessful. I guess it's time now to get some information out of Jessica. I quickly got dressed and made my way down to the bar to meet with Jessica. On the way there, I began to think of some questions to ask in order to pry any information I could out of her.

Having arrived at the bar a little early, I ordered a cocktail and sat there letting my mind wonder. I began to fantasize of what my life will be like away from the constant surveillance of the organization. I know I will not have the luxury of being able to stay in one place. My life will forever consist of being on the run. In a small way that was okay with me, but what would I do to pass the time? I have spent so many years training and following orders, and I am looking forward to having some freedom in my life once again. I must have been deep in thought, because I didn't see Jessica come up to the table.

"Svetlana?" She said when she stopped and stood in front of me before sitting in the seat across from me. "How are you today?"

"Oh, hello Jessica" I replied. "I'm doing well. How about you?"

"I'm a bit tired, but okay. I had a long night last night doing some research." She said.

"Research? What type of research, if you don't mind me asking?" I asked.

Was she searching me, or information pertaining to the summit meetings? If it is the former, I needed to take some measures to make sure she only finds what I want her to. If it was the latter, I could honestly care less. The summit meant absolutely nothing to me. I am here for one reason and one reason only. I just hope Jessica will be the key I need to get some information about Tripp. I have a sneaky suspicion that his name was a cover. This gut feeling, if true, will cause some issues for my investigation. I made a vow years ago that I would never take down a target until I found out all I could about him or her. Jessica may be my only chance to find out the information I needed before completing my mission.

"Nothing too specific. I've just been looking some stuff up about this summit. It seems like a new concept here." She replied. "What are your thoughts?"

"Well, it is a fairly new concept. They are trying to generate peace between so many gangs and major mob activity. It has proven to be a difficult and timely venture, but they seem to be beginning to make some headway." I said. I then picked up my cocktail and began to sip it.

"I did notice crime has decreased a little since they have been holding these summits. I guess peace takes time after so much time of terror and bullying from these gangs and mobs." She said before standing up. "Excuse me for a moment. I'm going to run to the bar to pick up a couple of menus and order a drink. Would you like me to order another cocktail for you?"

"That would be great. Thank you. I'm having a dry martini." I said before taking another sip of my drink.

"Great. I'll be right back." She replied with a smile.

I resumed my thoughts after she walked away. Now, not only did I have my fantasies of freedom, I had thoughts of ways to get the information I needed from dear sweet Jessica. I was still debating on whether or not to expel her or leave her alone. My orders were to take care of Tripp. I'm guessing the organization knew nothing about Jessica because she was not part of the job. "I'll just have to play that one by ear." I thought to myself. It was then that Jessica walked back over to the table with a martini in one hand, and a coffee in the other.

"Still feeling tired?" I asked.

"Yes and no." She replied. "This is an Irish coffee."

"I see. Have you ever been there? To Ireland I mean." I asked.

"Actually, yes I have. I grew up there. I had an older sister, but she died in an accident a few years ago." She said as tears began to well up in her eyes.

"I'm sorry for your loss. Were you two close?" I was beginning to feel sympathetic for her.

"We were for a long time. I must have done something wrong to hurt her, because she left and never came back." She said.

Wait. This story was starting to sound oddly familiar. I just brushed it off as coincidence and continued with the conversation and my questioning. "I'm sorry that happened. I'm sure it had nothing to do with you."

"What about you? Do you have any siblings?" She asked.

"No. It's just me." I lied. "So tell me about this guy you're with. What's his name again?"

"Oh, his name is Tripp. I'm his assistant, and here to take any notes that are needed or arrange any meetings while we are here. He's a diplomat trying to help make the peace stick between the mobs and gangs in our area." She said.

"I tried to search him last night, but couldn't find out any information. I was sent here by the council to find out information on all those attending these meetings." I lied again.

"Well he's new on the job. You wouldn't find much information about him on the internet yet." Jessica said.

At that point a waitress walked up to the table. "Good afternoon ladies. Are you ready to order?" She said.

Jessica and I both ordered a small salad. The waitress took our orders and walked away. I had some reservations about Jessica and Tripp. If he was so new to this position, why would the organization want him killed? I needed to find out some more information. Jessica seemed to blow off my questions about Tripp, and I knew I wouldn't get the information I needed from her. I needed to come up with a new plan. We continued with idle conversation while we had lunch.

"Jessica, it was a pleasure getting to know you. Good luck with the remainder of the summit meetings." I said as I began to get up from the table. I laid some cash down to cover my portion of the bill and said, "I hate to run, but I need to prepare for the meeting later on. I hope to see you later. I'd love to meet your boss."

"It's no problem. I'll look for you later in order to introduce you to Tripp. He really is a nice guy." She said as I gathered my jacket and purse.

"That would be wonderful." I said and walked away.

CHAPTER
NINE

"CIAN, IS THIS REALLY A GOOD IDEA? She's dangerous now. What if she doesn't recognize you? Are you really going to risk your life in order to try and get her back?"

"Tara, it will all work out. We just have to have faith that She's still in there somewhere. We just need to try to bring that part of her out and make her see that she is still loved."

I do have my reservations on this plan, but I need to get her back. I know it's been an extremely long time, but I need to keep my faith that our love is stronger than whatever it was that happened to Val. Tara has valid fears, as I was the one who practically raised her. I have become like a big brother to her.

This plan will have to work; I am literally betting my life on love. I can only hope that Val will recognize me before she attempts to kill me, or my fake identity rather. I need to build some sort of fake identity for Tara and myself, then call in the hit on myself. It took years for me to find out where Val went when she ran away. Tara and I finally tracked her down in a small town outside of Dublin, but she took off before we could attempt to reach her. That was the last time we heard of her until recently.

"I hope you're right about this, Cian." Tara said with a grim look on her face. "I can't lose you both." She added with tears beginning to well in her eyes.

"Tara, I promise everything will work out. I understand your reasons for worrying, but for now put it out of your mind and go rest." I attempted to reassure her.

Tara finally relinquished her stand on the matter and reluctantly walked up the stairs to her room. It wasn't long before I heard her door slam and could faintly hear her fall heavily on her bed. The house we were staying in was rather old, so the hard wood floors echoed every sound.

I spent most of the night trying to build fake profiles for Tara and myself. My first task was to brush up my fake identity. I choose the name Tripp Maseru, and decided to make him a dirty politician that says he's working to take down mob and gang activity when he is actually working with them. This should get the attention needed in order to have a certifiable hit called in on him.

Tara's identity would be, Jessica, Tripp's personal assistant. I knew I couldn't leave Tara behind, and with the dangers of this plan I needed her as backup in case I couldn't convince Val that it was me when the time came. I knew deep inside that if all else failed, Tara would be the one to bring things together. She was so confused for so long after Val took off on us. Out of that confusion, strength flourished and she became one of the strongest women I know. Aside from Val that is.

I can only imagine what the life Val lived all this time had done to her. I have no idea what she looks like now, so I decided to keep tabs on the list of attendees for the peace summit I planned to use to stage the assassination. To my surprise, I came across the name Svetlana Romanov. Next to the name was Val's picture. She had changed so much. You could tell by the look on her face in the picture that she wasn't totally there anymore. Val used to be so vibrant and full of life. Now it just appeared that she was an empty shell, tired of life, and just following the orders that she was given.

It was vital to the plan that Val be the hit man, or woman, for this job. I made sure to make the special request when I called in the hit.

———

"Thank you for calling Organization Solutions. How may I direct your call?" The female receptionist asked.

"I'm looking for a specialized solution to a problem." I replied.

"One moment, please. I'll direct your call." She said before putting me on hold briefly, then transferring my call.

"Specialized solutions, how can I help you?" The gentleman said.

"I have a problem that needs to be taken care of, and a special request" I replied.

"I need a name, date, and place." He said.

"Tripp Masru, the week of October 24, 2017 in Linz, Austria." I rattled off the information that was already sitting on the tip of my tongue.

"What was your special request?" He asked.

"I've heard that Val is one of your best. I'd like her to take care of this if possible." I was a bit nervous at the silence that followed from the other end of the line.

"Thank you for your call, sir. Everything will be taken care of." The man said before the line went dead.

I guess they aren't much for pleasantries. I thought to myself as I hung up the phone. Everything was set up. It was up to Tara and myself to convince Val that it was us before she killed me. She has been gone for so long, and I knew she wouldn't recognize her sister, or me, for that matter.

There was still a lot of planning to do before Tara and I set off for Austria, but I figured all of that could wait until tomorrow. For now, I just wanted to sit with a glass of scotch, a cigarette, and think about Val. As I poured the scotch, doubt and anxiety flooded through me. Was I doing the right thing for all of us? Putting Tara and myself in harm's way to save Val seemed like the craziest of ideas, but I can no longer sit and watch as Tara suffered. We both spent all these years worrying and wondering if we would ever see Val again. I have to do everything I can to get her back. That includes putting my own life on the line in order to do so.

I slowly picked up my glass of scotch and sat down heavily into my arm chair. I took slow long sip from my glass and let the alcohol burn slowly down my throat. After putting my glass on the small end table next to me, I picked up my cigarette case. I sat for a moment and twisted the personalized sterling silver case in my hand as I began to get lost in thought. I thought back to the very first time I saw Val at the orphanage. I knew right at that moment that I was in love with her. I guess you could say that it was truly love at first sight. After a few weeks together I knew I wanted to spend the rest of my life with her. It broke my heart the day Val ran away from the orphanage. I wasn't about to let her down though. No matter how much that day has caused me pain, I kept my promise to Val and watched after her sister as if she were my own.

I was snapped back into reality as Tara made her way down the stairs. I hadn't realized how long I had been sitting there engrossed in my thoughts. It was already approaching three a.m. in the morning.

"Cian, is everything okay?" Tara asked as she turned the corner and looked at me with a clear look of concern.

I looked at the cigarette case in my hand, then slowly looked up at her as I opened the case, pulled out a cigarette, and held the case up toward her. I'm sure by the look on my face Tara could tell that I had just been thinking about Val. Tara pulled a cigarette out of the case and sat on the couch closest to where I was sitting. I lit both of our cigarettes and we sat in silence for a few moments.

Tara must not have been able to handle the silence because she looked over at me and said, "we're going to get her back, Cian."

Her voice seemed a little shaky so I glanced over at her with a half-smile. It was then that I saw the tear slowly traveling down her right cheek. I knew then that no matter what doubts I had about this crazy plan I had come up with, I needed to keep a positive attitude. At this point it was hard to remember that I wasn't the only one with something to lose here. Tara was the one with the most to lose. If my plan failed, she would not only lose me, but she would also lose her sister.

I let my halfcocked smile widen a little more into a full closed lipped smile. "This is going to work, Tara." I said as I squeezed her hand lightly. I'm not sure if I was attempting to reassure Tara or myself.

I picked up my almost empty glass and asked Tara if she wanted something as I pushed myself up and out of my chair. She nodded her head and said, "I'll have whatever you're having."

I sluggishly walked over to the bar and poured two glasses of scotch, then walked back to where Tara was. I held out a glass to her then sat back down in the armchair. Neither of us wanted to talk, but we also didn't want to be alone. We just sat silently in each other's company. I continued with my thoughts of Val. I let myself imagine what she might be doing at this very moment. Or what she might be thinking about. With everything that she has been through, I wondered if she even remembered Tara and me.

I put my cigarette out in the crystal ashtray and pushed back into the chair activating the recliner. The mental exhaustion mixed with the alcohol was beginning to grip my body. I must have drifted off because the next sound I heard was the clinking of pots and pans in the kitchen. The sun was pushing its way through the curtains causing an ambient glow to encompass the living room.

I shifted my weight in the chair and could tell by the deep ache in my muscles that I had been in the same position for several hours. Tara must have heard me shuffling around in the chair, because the noise in the kitchen went quiet and moments later she emerged.

"I'm sorry. I didn't mean to wake you." She said.

I looked up at her and said, "It's okay. I need to get started with the plans." I winced as I leaned forward in the chair while using my legs to push the foot rest down. I sat for a moment before pulling a cigarette out of the case on the end table and lighting it. I took a long slow drag from it before standing up to stretch my stiff muscles.

"Are you hungry? I was just getting ready to make a late breakfast." Tara asked with an apologetic look. I could see she felt horrible about waking me up.

"Sounds good, Tara, thanks." I said with a smile that in itself showed the exhaustion still pulling at me. I excused myself and made my way upstairs to clean up. I was in desperate need of an extremely hot shower to wash away the mounting stress, and relax my stiff back muscles.

Tara had become quite the cock over the years. The unmistakable smell of bacon was flooding the house as I made my way back down stairs. Just as I planted my foot at the bottom of the stairs, Tara called out to me. "Cian, breakfast is done."

I had forgotten how hungry I really was. The smell of the bacon and eggs caused my taste buds to salivate on overdrive. I felt like I was all but drooling when I sat down at our small table and saw that Tara made one of my favorite meals, eggs in bacon baskets completed with Dubliner cheese grated over the top.

I looked up at Tara after I sat down and said, "this looks and smell amazing!"

"Thank you, Cian." She replied with a smile.

We sat and ate in silence. Neither of us wanted to say anything. Our stress levels were extremely high, and we both knew we could either lose everything or win back the person we both lost so long ago. No matter how broken Val is, I have to stay positive that I will be able to get through to her.

Once we were finished I slid my laptop from the case in the chair next to me and started working on our plans. The first item on my list was to buy plane tickets to Austria. It took a little while to find the right flight, then make sure I had two seats together. My plan was to have Tara meet up with her sister first, then I would invite her to have drinks in order to get close to her. I'm sure Val was coming up with a plan of her own similar to this. I'm sure she liked to get close to her targets at times, and I was hoping this was one of those times.

I hadn't realized that Tara had already cleared the table, and cleaned the kitchen. The next thing I knew she was standing next to me. I was still in the middle of typing out our ever growing list of things that we needed to do and will do once there. Tara stayed where she was until I finished and looked up at her.

"Sorry, I didn't mean to interrupt you. I'm headed to the store. Do you need anything while I'm out?" She asked.

"I can't think of anything right now, but we are going to need to go out and get some things in order to make some fake IDs and passports." I told her.

"Okay. I won't be out long. We can go when I get back if you're ready." She replied. I nodded, and then walked out the door.

After Tara left I decided it was time to get up and stretch. I also need another cigarette, so I walked into the living room where my cigarette case was still sitting on the end table next to my chair. I sat down and reclined back into the chair after picking up the silver case, pulled out a cigarette, and lit it.

I sat there thinking while Tara was gone. It was as if my heart was being pulled in several different directions at the same time. I was on my third cigarette when Tara finally came back. As soon as she walked in the door, I met her in the dining room. She put her bags on the table, and we were off to get the supplies needed to create our new IDs and passports.

It took some time to meet up with my guy that I was buying the passports from. We met at a small pub in town, and he was late as usual. I sat at a small table in the back corner of the room while Tara sat at the bar. He finally strolled in fifteen minutes late and leisurely walked over to the table where I was sitting.

"Tripp I assume?" He asked as he pulled out a chair and sat down across from me.

"That's right." I replied.

He opened the briefcase on the floor, pulled out a manila envelope, and placed it on the table in front of him.

"Do you have the payment?" He asked with a serious look on his face that would frighten anyone.

I knew this man was dangerous to deal with, but I was desperate. I played my part as best I could, so I looked him in the eye as I pulled the envelope full of cash from my jacket pocket and slid it across the table to him.

He took a moment to open the envelope and thumbed through the money inside. "It's all there." I reassured him.

He glanced up at me with a look that spoke for itself. It was clearly apparent that he didn't like my forwardness. He slid the manila envelope over to me and I opened it. I dumped the contents out on the table and glanced over them. There was an ID for Tripp Maseru and Jessica Thompson, as well as a passport for each.

"Thank you." I said as I offered my hand across the table for him to shake it.

He smirked then grabbed my hand and shook it. Before he stood up he assured me that the papers he made would pass through any security checks. That made me breathe a little easier. I nodded my approval as he turned to leave.

Once he was gone I stuffed the papers back into the envelope and gave Tara a look, then motioned for her to join me. She picked up the beer she'd been sipping, and sat down at the table. I could see she still had the worried look that she'd been harboring throughout the entire ordeal.

"I have to admit." She began. "I was worried about this meeting. That man is definitely someone I'd rather not deal with again."

"I'm with you there." I agreed.

We sat together for a while and finished our drinks before getting up to head home. The next month passed quickly, and before we knew it we were boarding a plane for Austria. It was finally time to see if all of our patience and planning would pay off.

CHAPTER
TEN

I THOUGHT ABOUT WHAT JESSICA SAID about her sister, and couldn't help the feelings of sorrow I felt for her. I was so angry with myself for allowing those feelings to surface. I have spent years teaching myself not to feel, and here I was becoming the weak little girl once again. Thoughts of my sister Tara began to resurface, and I felt a tear make its way down my cheek. I knew without a doubt that it was time to get out of this life of thoughtless killing.

I was so wrapped up in my thoughts that the knock on the door startled me. I picked up my small handgun from the dresser and walked over to the door. I placed the gun behind my back and cracked open the door. James was standing there all but inviting himself in.

"We don't need to pretend that you're not armed, Val." He said matter-of-factly.

"What the hell are you doing here, James?" I let my clear irritation show through my voice.

"Are you going to invite me in so we can talk? Or are you just going to shoot me?" He asked.

I opened the door enough for him to walk through, then closed the door behind him. There was no time like now to find out why James was here. I locked the door and turned to look toward James, who was now standing next to the window.

"You don't need that gun. I was sent here, but I'm more here as a favor for an old friend." He said without turning around to look at me.

"Get to the point." I said through my frustration at his cryptic talk. I still didn't trust his intentions, so I made sure to keep the gun in my hand.

"The Organization knows you intend to leave, Val." He began as he turned to look me in the eyes. "They sent me here to stop you by any means necessary. Please believe that is not my intention. I'm only here as a friend."

I looked at him in disbelief at what he just said. It wasn't in my nature to trust anyone anymore. "Do you expect me to believe you just came here to warn me?" I asked.

"If I hadn't agreed to come, they would've sent someone else, Val." He said with a sincere look on his face. "There's something else. Take care with this job. The person that called it in specifically requested you." He said as he sat on the foot of the bed.

"Are you worried about my judgement now, James?" I chuckled as I asked the question.

"All I'm saying is to watch your back." He retorted.

"You should know better than anyone that I am always expecting a trap. I'll be just fine." I was getting angry with his sudden concern for my well-being.

"Perhaps it would be better for all involved if you lost here. What I'm saying is, you get your man and for my sake I get mine." He offered as a solution to both of our problems.

"What do you propose?" I asked. For the first time during our conversation I was intrigued. It would be interesting to hear his plan to get us both out of this mess alive.

I could tell the wheels were spinning in his mind as he looked off towards the window. "I'm going to have to report back to the organization. Either I have to die, or you do." He began. "We need to come up with a way to get you out, alive."

He was beginning to make sense. If I wanted to make a clean break from the organization, I needed to die. "So what's our plan, James?" I asked.

"Once you've finished your job we will need the stage your death. That way I can report back to the organization with photos. We're going to have to make this look good though. They know how good you are, which is why they sent me." James said as he looked over at me.

He was right. He was one of the few people with the organization that could be a match for me with skill. We did need to make this look good, but how? I walked over to where James was sitting on the bed, and sat down next to him. I still didn't fully trust his intentions, so I kept the gun easily assessable in my hand. I knew he understood my reservations towards him. Since he was, after all, sent there to kill me.

I tried to imagine my life without having to be on the run, and being reunited with my sister without fearing for her safety. I had no idea if this plan would work well enough to get the organization off my back for good. I hadn't really thought about what I would do with my life once I was out. How can I have a normal life? I have no idea what that meant anymore. The word normal hasn't been a part of my vocabulary in so long.

"I'm meeting with Tripp this evening. I've already met and had a conversation with his assistant, Jessica. I need to find out a little more about this man. I haven't been able to find out anything about him. It's as if he never existed before this week." I began. "I have more questions about that man than I have answers." I said.

"And you were wondering why I told you to be careful on this one. This could be a new agent sent by the organization in case I failed." He said with a serious look on his face.

He had a point. Tripp Maseru didn't seem to exist until just before this week. I needed to meet with this man to try and find out all that I can about him. If he was sent by the organization, it would definitely make my job much easier. I couldn't get over the nagging questions in my mind of who these people were, and who, if anyone, sent them.

"Meet me here in the morning." I told James. "I'll find out what I need to know about Tripp tonight, then we can finish going over our plan."

I'm still not sure how I was going to fish the information I needed out of Tripp, but something was better than nothing. I only hope that he would be forthcoming with information, or at least the information that I needed. Either way, it was time for me to get ready to meet Tripp downstairs for dinner.

James agreed to meet me in the morning in order to go over and perfect our plan. He put his hand on my shoulder, and slowly stood up from his seated position on the bed.

"Take care, Val." He said as he walked towards the door, unlocked it and left the room.

I sat for a moment longer and went over some of the questions I wanted to ask Tripp later that evening. There were just some questions that did not need to be avoided. I needed to know who this guy and his assistant was. I took my time sitting there with my thoughts. There was still some time before I needed to get ready to head downstairs.

While sitting there I couldn't help the thoughts of my sister that hijacked my mind. It wasn't just Tara that came to the forefront of my memories, I began to think of Cian as well. I still remember the day I left like it was yesterday. I could still see the pain on Cian's face as I turned to run away, and the vow to watch over Tara as he called out after me.

I glanced over at the digital clock next to the bed and realized that I needed to get myself ready to go. I decided to put on a nice dress and donned my makeup. The dress I chose was all black with a type of 'V' neck in order to show my cleavage. The dress connected behind my neck leaving the back open. There was a slit on one side that opened the bottom of the dress and stopped at my thigh. My thought process was to look appealing enough in order to throw Tripp off enough to hopefully get some answers.

Once I was ready, I stopped in front of the mirror and stared at myself. "Okay, Val. You can do this." I said to myself. "You just need to find out as much as you can about Tripp." I continued. "This is it, one last chance." Tomorrow I was planning to complete this job and finally liberate myself from the organization.

James was going to help me disappear forever by making the organization think that he had killed me. My life would forever change in the next day or so. I still had no plans for my future, and couldn't afford to be distracted by thoughts of what would or wouldn't transpire.

"Okay." I said out loud as I picked up my clutch that was laying on the dresser next to the television. I opened it and placed my small twenty-two caliber handgun and key card for my room in it, then walked out the door.

The elevator ride to the lobby seemed to last a lifetime as I was in there with a rather large man with terrible personal hygiene. The elevator seemed to fill with his unbearably strong musk by each passing moment. I stood in the far back corner of the elevator wanting to hold my breath. Once the indicator bell went off signaling we had finally made it to the lobby, I don't think I have ever been happier. The large gentleman stood off to the side as he put his arm in front of the elevator door to keep it from closing.

I looked at him with a soft grin and said thank you as I walked past him and into the lobby. I waited until I was in the bar before breathing a sigh of relief. A moment later the host walked over to me.

"How can I help you this evening, miss?" He asked.

"I'm meeting a gentleman by the name of Tripp here." I replied.

"Yes ma'am, he is here waiting. If you will just follow me." He said as he began walking towards the corner of the bar. "If I may be so bold as to say, you look very stunning this evening."

"That is bold of you to say." I said.

"I apologize. I mean no disrespect miss." He recanted. "Mr. Maseru is waiting right this way." He said as he pointed to a table in the corner.

I smiled and nodded. "Thank you." I said as I walked past the host and toward the small table.

"My pleasure miss." The host replied as he turned and walked back towards the entrance of the bar.

I made my way over to the table where Tripp was seated. I weaved my way through the maze of tables until I was finally standing in front of Tripp. He glanced up at me with an inquisitive look.

"Good evening, I'm Svetlana, you must be Tripp." I said as I shifted my weight from one leg to the other.

"Yes ma'am." He began as he pushed himself away from the table and stood up while extending his hand to shake mine. "It's very nice to finally meet you. Jessica mentioned you wanted to meet with me."

He walked around the table and pulled out a chair, then offered for me to sit. I accepted his offer and placed my clutch on the table before sitting down as he pushed my chair in towards the table.

"Thank you, Mr. Maseru, and Jessica was correct. I've seen you at the summit meetings, and thought we should meet." I said.

"What do you say we order some drinks and get to know one another." He replied.

"Perfect." I thought to myself. I hope he will be willing to offer up some information about himself and his assistant. It didn't concern me that they didn't seem to exist until just before this summit. I was extremely proficient at my job, and if they were sent by the organization to kill me, I wouldn't go down without a fight. Tripp called the waitress over.

"Good evening." She began. "What can I get for you?"

"I'll have an Irish coffee." I said.

"Yes ma'am. And you sir?" She asked as she looked towards Tripp.

"I'll have a scotch on the rocks." Tripp replied.

"I'll be right back with your order." She said as she turned towards the bar and walked away.

Tripp had an inquisitive look as I ordered, and I could tell he was trying to figure me out. I decided I would beat him to the punch and ask the first of the many questions I had for him.

"So, Mr. Maseru, where are you from?" I asked.

"I'm from a small town in France. How about you Ms. Romanov?" He said.

"I live on the coast in Magadan, Russia." I replied. "It is very beautiful there in the winter." I added. "What brings you here for the summit?" I asked.

"I'm working with my government to help control gang activity." He replied as it was evident he gave me a once over type of look.

"I didn't know there were issues with gangs in France." I said as the waitress returned with our drink orders.

"Uh, yes, there is a new gang wreaking havoc in Paris. There have been many robberies and killings." He retorted.

Did he just stammer with his answer? Hmm…. "I had not heard anything about this travesty. What's the name of the gang?" I asked.

"They call themselves Kane. They are extremely well organized, almost military like." He said.

"Really?" I said in total and complete disbelief at what he just said. I had extensive knowledge of gangs and mafia. After all, I was sent to kill a large majority of their leaders over the years. "So tell me some of your background Mr. Maseru. Do you have any military experience?" I asked. That would be one of the fastest ways to gain some information about him if I was unable to get him to open up.

"I'm afraid not. I'm just a political advisor who worked his way up through the ranks the hard way." He replied.

I was making sure to take into account his facial expressions and body language as he answered my questions. There were a few times it seemed apparent that he was lying, then trying to cover his tracks with his next answers. Who was this man and his assistant? At this point I could hear James' warning ringing in my head. If he didn't know who they were, then I had to be careful.

The waitress made her way back over to our table. "Can I get you another drink?" She asked. She was clearly pointing the question at both of us as our glasses were empty.

"Nothing for me. Thank you." I replied.

"Sir, what about you?" She asked as she looked towards Tripp.

"No thank you." He said.

The waitress nodded in response then walked away. I had a

feeling that I gathered enough information about Tripp to conduct another search. I decided it was time to excuse myself for the evening. If this couple were from the organization, their cover was extremely weak and had way too many holes in it. The thing that annoyed me the most was that I still had no idea who they were, and worst yet, why the organization sent me specifically.

"Mr. Maseru, I hate to cut this evening short, but I must get some rest before tomorrow's meeting." I said as I opened my clutch and pulled out enough money to pay for my drink and a generous tip.

"Of course, Ms. Romanov. I hope you have a good evening. It was a pleasure getting to know you this evening." He replied as he began to push his chair away from the table to stand up.

I closed my clutch and pushed myself away from the table enough to where I could stand up. In a gentleman like manner, he stood up at the same time I did. I offered my hand to him in order to shake his, but in response he took hold of my hand and gently kissed the top of it.

"Thank you for a nice evening." I said as I retrieved my hand, and turned to walk away.

CHAPTER
ELEVEN

OKAY, TIME TO FIND OUT WHO YOU and your assistant are Mr. Maseru. I said to myself as I sat down at the small desk in my room and opened my laptop. I first used a general search engine to look up Tripp using the little bits of information I gathered earlier. If I can't find any information this time, I will have to resort to more drastic measures.

One way or another I am going to find out who these two are, and who, if anyone, sent them. I am too close to being free to slip up now. I can't afford to have anyone think they can cash in on my life. I can't help but wonder if the organization, since they know about my plans to leave, sent more than one contractor to kill me. James sure wasn't any help in the matter. He swears that he was the only one they sent after me.

I only hope he knows that I will not hesitate to kill him if he is lying to me. I figured another meeting with him would be a necessity after I finish my searches for Tripp and his assistant. Something in me hoped that I would finally find something on them. It would definitely make my job a little easier.

My first search came back with no results, so I decided to hack into the French government website and search their records. Hacking the French government was going to take some time so I figured now would be as good a time as any to employ some help from James. This way I can forcibly confront him for any information he may have about the organization, and any other contractors they may have sent out after me.

I walked over to the bedside table where the phone was sitting, picked up the receiver and dialed his room. The phone only rang a couple of times before he answered.

"Yes?" He answered.

"Not one for phone etiquette, huh?" I teased.

"Oh, any new information after your meeting, Val?" He replied clearly recognizing my voice.

"I need your help, James. Are you up for it?" I asked.

"You must really be stuck if you're calling me." He said.

"I don't want to hear it, James. Are you up for it or not?" I said making my annoyance clear.

"Yeah, yeah. Try some decaf, Val. I'll be there in a few." He said seeming to understand the anger and annoyance I was conveying.

I didn't give him a chance to say anything before I put the receiver back on the hook. This whole situation was wearing on me, and to be honest, pissing me off. All I wanted right now was a clean way out, and it seemed that Tripp and his assistant Jessica were complicating things. If I couldn't find any information on them, I would just remove the complication by any means necessary.

The more I thought about my situation the angrier I got. As a means to calm myself down a little before James got to my room, I stood up from the bed and walked to the sink in the bathroom. I turned the cold water on and let it run for a moment before filling my hands and splashing the cold liquid on my face. I pulled the white embroidered towel from the shelf next to the sink and dabbed my face with it.

After cooling myself off and subsequently waking myself up a little, I threw the towel on the counter next to the sink and walked over to the mini refrigerator next to the small desk. I opened the small door and pulled out a small bottle of whisky, opened it, and emptied the contents into my mouth. It took a couple of hard swallows to get the smoky liquid down, but the liquor had an instant heating effect on my body.

I had just thrown the empty bottle into the trash when there was a knock at the door. I opened the top drawer of the small dresser underneath the television and grabbed my small nine-millimeter before walking over to the door.

"Who is it?" I asked through the door.

"It's James, Val." The male voice replied.

I slowly opened the door enough for James to walk inside. I grabbed James by the collar of his shirt and pushed him against the wall pressing my forearm into his neck and kicked the door closed.

"Tell me everything you know about the organization." I began while pressing the gun against his temple. "Who else have they sent, James?" I demanded.

"Jesus, Val!" He said while holding his hands up. "Why don't you tell me what the hell is going on, and put that damn gun down."

"James, I swear to god I'll pull this trigger if you don't answer my question." I began. "I know you're not the only person watching me. Who else have they sent?" I asked again.

"Okay. Okay. Damn!" He said. "Once the organization found out you were planning to leave, they put out a hit on you. The only other person I've seen is Savanna."

What the hell? Savanna was like family to me while at the academy. I had a hard time believing that she would be willing to kill me. Had I allowed myself to be set up?

"Val, listen to me." James said. "We need to work on the problem at hand. You need to find out who this Tripp fella and his lady friend is. Then we can end this for good. I will help you any way I can."

I found myself at a crossroads, and knew I couldn't trust anyone, much less my judgement right now. I had so many questions swimming in my mind. Was James planning to betray me? Did he lie to be about Savanna being here? But most of all, who the hell was Tripp Maseru and Jessica?

"Can you please put the gun down, Val?" James asked.

"Not just yet." I replied. "Is Savanna staying at this hotel?" I asked.

"I honestly don't know, Val. I saw her for the first time tonight at the bar." He said. "I went down there to make sure you were alright. I don't trust this Tripp fella, and neither should you."

"James, you of all people should know I am more than capable of taking care of myself." I began. "To be completely honest. I don't trust you either. Hence the loaded gun pressed against your head right now." I said as I pressed the barrel even further into his temple.

"Come on, Val. If I was going to kill you I would've done it already. I came here tonight because you said you needed my help. I know you don't trust me, but I am on your side." He said.

I could see some truth displayed in his expression so I removed the gun from his head and put it to his chest. "James, I swear to god, if you betray me I will kill you." I said matter-of-factly.

"I believe you, Val. Now, can we get to work? Or are we going to spend the rest of the night stancing here with you pointing a gun at me?" James asked making it clear he was there to help me. The only question was for how long.

I let him go and took a step back. "I need you to hack into the French government mainframe and search for this guy." I said as I lowered my gun and motioned toward my laptop.

"Oh, is that all? I thought you were going to ask me to do something difficult." He said jokingly.

"Enough, James. Can you do it?" I asked annoyed at his sudden need to joke around.

James walked over to the desk and sat down. He intertwined his fingers and pushed the palms of his hands towards the computer. What is it with men forever being immature? I walked over to the small refrigerator and pulled another small bottle of whisky out and offered one to James, who declined.

"Suit yourself." I said as I walked over to the bed and sat down behind James. I sat the gun down on the bed next to me and opened the small bottle of liquor.

I must have had three more bottles of various spirits before saying, "Jesus, James! What the hell is taking so long?"

"I'm not exactly checking my email here, Val. This takes time." He said seemingly annoyed by my impatience.

He took a brief moment to stretch his neck before his fingers went back to work on the keyboard again. He seemed to be genuinely working hard to help me, but that by no means meant that I trusted him. A learned habit that comes with the trade.

"I'm breaking through the last firewall now." James said as he turned his head slightly in my direction.

He was already in the system and searching for Tripp by the time I made it to his side. Our first search returned with less than desired results, so we moved on to another branch of the government. After searching various branches of the French government James looked over at me almost apologetically.

"Val, I'm starting to think this guy really doesn't exist." He said.

"Damn it!" I half yelled out of frustration.

"I know that look, Val. What are you planning to do?" James asked.

"I'm going to finish this." I began. "Tomorrow. Then you and I will do what needs to be done."

CHAPTER
TWELVE

I HAD A FEW MORE DRINKS after James left my room. Somehow drinking calms me down, yet lets me hold onto my anger. My strong Irish blood thankfully allows me to not only hold my liquor, but frees me from the morning hangovers.

I woke up still furious about the knowledge that Tripp Maseru and Jessica did not exist. Their identities were created for some reason, and I was hell bent on finding out what that reason was today. I had yet to form a plan of attack. That was the first and foremost item on today's agenda. Right after I took a hot shower of course.

I sat up in the bed, which seemed a little difficult considering I spent the better part of the night hacking the French government mainframe with James. After finding dead ends on the mainframe, James and I talked over our plan to make the organization believe he succeeded in his mission to kill me.

Once on my feet, I stretched then made my way to the bathroom. I turned the water on in the shower as hot as it would go, and got in. The heat of the water created a welcomed relief to my tense muscles. I just stood there as long as I dared letting the water cascade down the back of my neck, shoulders, and back.

I lost track of the time while in the shower. I hadn't realized how long I was in there until I heard my cell phone going off. The call had to have been from James. Part of today's plans were for James to find out what room Tripp and Jessica were staying in.

If it was a fight they wanted, then it was a fight they would get. One way or the other the truth was going to come out. I planned to find who they were, and why they were here once and for all. I had a gut feeling that it would come down to me or them. Even through the disharmony within myself, my mission must be completed.

I decided to let my cell ring, and finished my shower. After spending so much time beneath the hot water, the rest of my shower was rushed due to fading heat of the water. After getting out of the shower, I dried myself off and wrapped a towel around me then walked over to the counter where my makeup bag was.

I took my time putting my makeup on, making sure to hide the dark circles that formed underneath my eyes from the lack of sleep. I waited until I finished doing my hair to call James back. I picked up my cell and scrolled down to his name and pressed the send button. The phone rang a few times before he finally answered.

"Val?" The voice on the other end asked.

"Yeah, James it's me. Did you find out which room they are staying in?" I asked.

"Yes." He replied. "They are staying in room 1315. Watch your six, Val."

"Thanks for the information, and the warning, James. You of all people should know I know how to take care of myself." I said matter-of-factly then hung up the phone before he could say anything else.

Okay, now that I knew where they were it was time to come up with a plan. I decided to forego the meeting set for today in order to plan my form of attack. I was conflicted on whether or not to invite them to my room to talk or go to theirs. Either way, this was going to end today.

I got dressed in a pair of cargo pants and a tank top. My thought process while doing so was to be able to move agilely if I had to take on them both on at the same time. Once dressed I walked over to my desk and sat down in front of my laptop. After opening it, I waited until it booted up. I needed to plan my escape so I could leave as soon as James and I finished our business arrangement.

After getting ready I put on some light makeup. I really wanted to find Savanna, and find out why she was here. I know I didn't want to fight and kill the only friend I had, but if it had to be done, who better than me? It was still early and I wanted to catch Tripp and Jessica before they made their way down to the summit meeting for the day.

After donning my makeup, I opened the top drawer of the small dresser and picked up the small gun I had hidden there, checked to make sure it was loaded with a round in the chamber, and placed in just behind my back inside my pants. I shuffled some of the clothes around and found the two clips I had there. I placed them in the left leg pocket of the cargo pants, then walked over to the small bedside table and opened the drawer there. I had loaded nineteen eleven there in case I needed it. I picked it up, made sure it was loaded with a round in the chamber as well, and placed it in my pants next to the small nine-millimeter. I had two more loaded clips sitting next to it, and picked those up to put in the other leg pocket. I know it seemed like overkill, but I was looking at two armed targets that I was about to confront.

I double checked to make sure I had everything I needed before opening the door to make sure the hallway was empty before stepping out. I had a short walk to the room number that James had given me earlier that morning. I wasn't concerned in the least how he retrieved the information, but I hoped it was accurate. I closed the door to my room while keeping my back to the wall. I couldn't afford anyone walking up behind me while having guns out in the open for all to see.

I stealthily moved down the halls putting my back to the wall each time I saw someone walking towards me down the hallway. Once they were out of site, I began my track towards room 1315. There was a crossroads in the hallway coming up in front of me, and once there, I stopped to see not only which way I should go, but looked both directions to make sure no one was walking my way.

Once I made sure the coast was clear I looked at the board on the wall that directed guest to room numbers. "Okay." I said quietly. "A right turn and I'm there." I was almost certain that Tripp would be the one answering the door, and prepared myself for that. This hallway ran two directions, so I pulled my tank top over the guns stuffed in the back of my pants. I couldn't take the chance of someone seeing me and causing a panic.

The hallway I was on had an outside wall on the left-hand side, and the rooms on the right. I had about five doors to go before I was at my destination. During my walk past the last few doors I started to go over my plan again in my mind. I wanted answers, but if I had to fight, I was ready. Actually, I was more than ready.

It wasn't long before I was standing outside of room number 1315. I looked around to make sure that nobody was coming down the either side of the hallway, then pulled the small nine-millimeter from my waistband. I double checked that it had a load in the chamber no matter who answered the door.

I slowly made my way down the corridor, making sure that I wasn't seen, until I found my destination. Before knocking on the door, I pulled the small nine millimeter from my waistband, and pulled the slide back slightly to insure there was a round in the chamber. Insured that I was ready, I balled my fist up and knocked on the door a couple of times. I could clearly hear Jessica's voice call out.

"One moment please." She said.

"Make sure you know who it is before you open the door." Tripp called out after her.

"Who's there?" She asked through the door.

"Room service." I answered.

I heard the clip lock move that was located at the top of the door, then the door opened. I quickly pushed myself inside and kicked the door closed behind me. I grabbed Jessica by the shirt with my left hand, then threw her against the wall closest to the door. I pressed the gun to her head, and could see Tripp move from around the corner out of the corner of my eye.

"One more step and she's dead." I said forcefully.

"Okay. Okay, but you don't understand." He said

"Just tell her!" Jessica called out. "You're not the one with a gun to your head."

"Tell me what?" I demanded.

"We aren't who you believe we are." Tripp began. "I'm Cian and this is Tara." He said as he first pointed at himself then Jessica.

"Impossible!" I yelled out of anger.

"It's true." He said while holding his hands out in front of him in the manner you would to calm someone down. "This was the only way we knew how to find you."

"You're lying!" I replied.

Jessica spoke up then. "Do you remember the day that mom

and dad died?" She asked nervously.

"What about my parents' death?" I asked her not letting up on my grip or the gun in my hand. "You could've looked up the newspaper clipping about it." I added.

"True." She began. "But what wouldn't be in there is where we hid during the robbery."

I took a moment and looked her in the eyes. There was a tear forming there, then fell down her cheek. I began to doubt myself. I wanted to find my sister once I was freed from the organization. I had no intentions of bringing her into all of this.

While keeping my eye on her face and Tripp, Cian, or whoever the hell was standing on the other side of the room in sight. "You'll say anything in order for me to not pull the trigger on this gun."

"Think about it." She began. "Where did we hide?"

"Where?" I asked hoping that she would be wrong.

She looked me dead in the eye and said, "we hid in the back of the bathroom closet while the thieves destroyed our lives."

No one else knew this part of my past. I had never told anyone about this. Not even Cian. Was this really my sister and Cian? I moved the gun from Tara's head and fell hard to my knees with tears flowing down my face. Tara bent down and wrapped her arms around me crying as well.

"Val." She said through her tears. "We have been looking for you for a very long time. This was the only way we knew how to get to you."

I couldn't quite get over the fact that I held a loaded gun to my sister's head, and was ready to kill her. Not only that, but I was more than ready to kill Cian. I didn't want them mixed up in my mess, but here they were. I knew they weren't going to like what had to happen in order for me to get out of the organization for good.

"We all need to talk." I said through my emotion, which was something I hadn't felt in years.

I talked for what seemed like hours about the plan that James and I came up with. I could see the tears streaming down Tara's face as she knew this was not going to be easy. Cian finally spoke after I finished divulging my plan of escape.

"Do you really need to go through with this?" He asked.

"Yes." I began. "The organization needs to believe that I'm dead in order for me to be free of them."

I could see the pain on his face, yet I continued. "Sure, they will send contractors to make sure I'm truly gone, but that is nothing I can't handle."

"Val, you're not alone in this anymore." Cian said.

I looked over and watched as Tara nodded in agreement. I couldn't risk either of their lives, but knew they were right. There was no way I could keep them safe any longer.

CHAPTER
THIRTEEN

AFTER WHAT SEEMED LIKE HOURS of catching up and going over the necessary plans, I decided it was time to move the group to my room. I waited impatiently while Cian and Tara packed their bags. As I looked at them, I went over the plan over and over again in my mind. My only concern at the moment was Savanna. Was she really here? If so, why? I couldn't allow myself to believe she was here to kill me. The too sweet girl I once knew, and who helped me through the training at the academy more than she knew.

Before dealing with James, I needed to find Savanna and talk to her. There were just way too many questions that needed answers. Once Cian and Tara were packed and ready to go, we made our way down the hallway until we were finally at my room. I pulled the keycard from my back pocket and inserted it into the locking mechanism. Once the light turned green indicating the lock was disengaged. I turned the handle and slowly opened the door. James had already broken into my room once, and I wanted to be sure he wasn't sitting in there waiting. A fight was the last thing I wanted right now, and I knew if James saw me with Cian and Tara there would be hell to pay until he knew the truth.

I put one hand up towards Cian and Tara to indicate that I wanted them to wait a moment behind me. Once I knew they understood I pulled one of the guns from my waistband and eased into the room. I first checked the bathroom, then moved into the area of the room where the bed and desk were. Once I made sure there wasn't anyone there, I put the gun back in my waistband and motioned for Cian and Tara to come in.

Tara came in and sat down on the bed before laying back and letting out a long and heavy sigh. Cian walked past the bed and put their bags down on the floor next to the window.

"Val, what are you thinking about?" Cian asked.

I must have had a clear look of concern and trepidation. "I was told that an old friend from the organization was here." I told him.

"Okay. So why would that worry you like this?" He asked.

"Cian, there are many things about my world that you just don't understand. This friend could either be here to help me or kill me." I said. "I can't risk having something happen to you or Tara."

"So, what are you planning?" Cian asked.

"I must find her and find out why she is here, or even if she is here for that matter." I began. "You and Tara stay here. Do not for any reason answer the door. I'll be back as soon as I can." I said as I made my way toward the door.

I gave Cian a quick nod and walked out the door. I quickly made my way to the elevator and pushed the down arrow multiple times. Once the doors opened I rushed in and pushed the button for the lobby. The elevator seemed to take forever once again as it made its way slowly downward. I was relieved when the doors finally opened in the lobby.

I stepped out of the elevator and quickly made my way to the front desk. If Savanna was staying here I was going to find out and invite her for a drink. There was a young man working at the desk.

He looked up at me from his computer and asked, "yes ma'am. How can I assist you?"

I pulled out my phone and opened the photos application. I quickly flipped through the photos to the one I had of Savanna. Once I had the picture up, I showed it to him and asked, "Have you seen this young lady?"

"Yes ma'am." He answered. "She's sitting at the bar as we speak."

This is easier than I thought. "Thank you." I said to the gentleman at the desk. I then turned away from the desk, and made my way to the bar.

Once inside the bar I looked around and spotted Savanna sitting at a small table by the window. I leisurely weaved through the tables, and made my way to where she was sitting. I stopped and stood next to her table and asked, "may I join you?"

She jumped a little at the sound of my voice, and I could tell she recognized my voice. She slowly looked up at me and said, "Val?"

I nodded my head at her then looked at the chair across from her. I had no idea how this conversation would go, so I made sure I was ready for anything. I didn't want to have to kill the only friend I've ever really known, but I would if it came to that.

"Have a seat." She finally said after the initial shock of me standing there wore off. "How have you been?" She asked as I pulled the chair out and sat down.

"I've been okay." I began. "Busy with work. How about you?" I asked.

"Oh, you know, busy with this and that." She said while shifting in her seat.

It was at that moment that I stuck my hand in the right-side cargo pocket of my pants and took hold of my gun. "So what brings you here, Savanna?" I asked. I had played enough games the last few days, and was pretty fed up with the secrets and lying.

She gave me an apprehensive look, clearly knowing that I knew about the organization's plans to get rid of me. She just shook her head, then looked down without saying anything.

"Savanna, I need to know why you're here. Did they send you for me?" I said with a clear sound of annoyance in my voice.

"Listen, Val." She began while keeping her eyes on the martini glass in front of her. "Yes they sent me, I came for you. You have to know I would never do anything to hurt you." She finally looked up at me with an apologetic look when she said that last part.

She must have known that in our line of business that I didn't trust anyone. That included acquaintances and friends. She glanced down at my right side, then said, "Val, you don't need that with me. I'm not going to do anything to hurt you. I just came to let you know that the organization is on to you."

"You must have known that I would know that the moment I decided to get out." I said.

She looked at me dead in the eyes, and I swear I could almost read her mind. "Yes." She said while still keeping her eyes on mine. "Just watch your back, Val." She concluded.

All I could do was nod my head in agreement. This whole situation had me a little stressed, and to be honest, extremely pissed off. Part of me was glad that Cian and Tara had never given up on me, but now we were all in danger. This was the very thing I was trying to avoid ever since that day they found me in Ireland. My plan has to work. I have to get us out of this alive and mostly in one piece.

Savanna slid a piece of paper across the table towards me. As I slid my hand over to grab the paper from her, she grabbed my hand. I have to admit it startled me a little. She looked me dead in the eye and said, "Val, I really have missed you. This is my private number. I'm always here if you need me. I really hope you believe me, and know that you can trust me."

She let go of my hand, and I could swear I could see tears welling up in her eyes. I could tell from the pure emotion on her face that I could trust her. I folded the paper a couple of times and slid it into the front pocket of my pants.

I looked at Savanna and slowly moved my hand across the table towards her. She slid her hand towards mine while keeping her eyes on mine. Our hands met and we gripped each other. It was difficult to allow the emotions welling up inside of me to show.

"Thank you, Savanna. I've missed you as well." I finally said as a tear, no matter how hard I tried to hold it back, fell from my eye and made its way down my cheek.

"I just hope you have a really good plan to get out of this." She said.

"I do." I said as I brushed the wetness from my face with my free hand. "I just hope it works the way I want it to."

Savanna's emotions got the better of her, and tears were free flowing down her face. "I don't want anything bad to happen to you, Val. I know that this is not going to be an easy out for you." She said. "Just take care of yourself."

"I will, Savanna." I said as a waitress walked over to our table.

"Can I get you anything, ma'am?" The waitress asked.

"No." I said to her. "I'm not staying. I was just saying hello to an old friend."

She looked over at Savanna and asked, "can I get you anything else?"

"Yes." Savanna replied. "I'll have another martini."

"Yes ma'am." The waitress said then turned and walked away.

"It was really nice to see you again." I said to Savanna. "I really need to get going."

"Likewise, Val." Savanna replied. "I really hope to see you again." She added.

I nodded as I stood up. I then offered my hand across the table in order to shake hers. She took hold of my hand, for what I hoped wasn't the last time, and briefly shook my hand. I brushed the tear away that escaped my eye as I turned away from her and walked towards the elevator.

CHAPTER
FOURTEEN

I COULDN'T HAVE BEEN HAPPIER that I was the only person in the elevator after my talk with Savanna. Emotion had gotten the better of me as my eyes betrayed me, and tears free flowed down my cheeks.

"Pull yourself together!" I said aloud to myself. I took a couple of struggled deep breaths. I needed to be strong now more than ever. I've been through so much worse than what was about to come in order to complete my plan to make the organization think James had killed me, but I wasn't sure how Cian, or Tara for that matter, would react.

I have to get my emotions back in check. I had hoped to execute my plan tonight, but I needed some time to gather myself now. I also wanted more time with Cian and Tara before having to go to a hospital a few towns over for the injuries I was about to sustain. My plan was to use one of my identities in order to get back to Ireland.

I was glad that the elevators in this hotel were unusually slow. I used that time wisely to get myself emotionally in check enough to pull my cellphone out of my pocket. I flipped through my contacts and found James' number. I touched the screen on his name, then again on the picture of a phone to place the call. The phone rang a couple of times before he picked up.

"Hello?" The voice on the other end said.

"James? It's Val." I said.

"Is everything set?" He asked.

"Yeah." I replied. "We're on for tomorrow."

"Sounds good. I'll stop by first thing in the morning." He said.

"See you then." I said and touched the button to end the call.

Just as I hung up with James the elevator doors opened on my floor. I slowly walked to my room, making sure to give myself enough time to fully regain my composure. I took a deep breath as I reach my door, then pulled the keycard from my back pocket. I slowly inserted the card into the lock of the door, then removed it. As soon as the green light indicated that the lock was disengaged, I pushed down on the door handle then slowly pushed the door open.

Tara was lying on the bed sleeping while Cian was sitting at the desk using my laptop. He looked up at me and said, "everything okay?"

"Yes. Why do you ask?" I replied. I could only assume he could see the redness in my eyes from the tears that were shed in the elevator.

"Did you find your friend?" He asked.

"I did." I was trying to keep my answers short. It was a terrible habit formed from years with the organization. I hated treating Cian like this.

"Val, I know you've had a hard life all these years, but Tara and I are here for you." He began as he stood up from the desk chair. "I hope that one day you will come to trust us again."

"Cian, I have never been happier to see you and Tara. You're right about me having lived a hard life. I have been inches from death more times than I can count, and in those times all I could think about was you and Tara." I said. "Getting out of this is not going to be an easy task. We need to come up with a plan in order to get out of this hotel and to a hospital a couple of towns over."

"Wait what?" He interrupted. "What do you mean? Why a hospital?" He asked.

I could see the clear concern on his face, but he had to understand the stakes. At the moment I was glad Tara was asleep during this conversation. Although, she was going to have to find out the gory details sooner than later, and I hated that for her.

I kept my eyes on Cian's and said, "the organization needs to think I'm dead in order for me to be free of them. Otherwise they will keep sending people to kill me." I looked down at the floor in order to hide the emotion that was building inside of me, then continued. "I have a friend from the organization that was sent to kill me. He has agreed to help me get out. We have come up with a plan, but I promise you it will not be pretty sight."

I glanced up at Cian in time to see his face contort to a look of pain. Tears welled up in his eyes and after a few minutes he spoke.

"Val, is there no other way? I just got you back, and can't bear the thought of losing you again." He began as he started walking towards me. "It took so long to calm Tara down after you left. I kept my promise to you, and looked after her as if she were my own sister. What am I supposed to do if you don't make it through this?" He asked.

"Cian, I understand how hard this must be for you." I said while trying to show some sense of assertiveness.

"Do you?" He asked clearly annoyed. "You have no clue what Tara and I went through after you left."

"I'm sorry. This is the only way. You have to understand that. I need you to believe that I will get through this." I couldn't stop the tears that began to fall down my face. I have been through so much, but have never felt this helpless.

I hated this whole situation. Not just for me, but for Tara and Cian as well. They were going to have to witness a horrific form of brokenness for me.

I walked past Cian and moved toward the window. I stood there with my back towards the window, and for a while neither of us said anything. Exhaustion and emotion got the better of me, and I slowly slid down the wall and onto the floor. I stretched my legs out and pulled my small handgun from my cargo pocket. I placed it next to me on the floor, then glanced up at Cian whose glance followed me to my position on the floor.

He walked over and sat down next to me on the floor. I couldn't help but to lean over and put my head on his shoulder. The love I felt for him while we were in the orphanage didn't seem to diminish over the years. I think I loved him more now for the bravery he had shown by coming for me.

I have to admit I was angry at the fact that he put himself and my sister in grave danger by being here, but I would gladly give my life to protect them both. I looked up at Cian who lifted his left hand slowly and brushed the tears from my face.

"Val, I have loved you since the first time I laid eyes on you." He began. "That has never changed." He concluded as he lifted my chin and kissed me softly on the lips.

He wrapped his arms around me as we continued our kiss. I never allowed myself to feel so vulnerable, but I also felt a sense of safety while sitting there in his arms. It wasn't long before I heard a shuffle coming from the bed. I looked up to see Tara sitting up and looking at Cian and I.

"Wow!" She said. "That is a sight for sore eyes. I see you two have made up." She said with a slight chuckle.

I looked over at Cian, and he gave a quick nod of his head. It was time to let Tara in on the plan. I knew she wasn't going to like it, and would react in the same manner, if not worse, as Cian.

I looked back over at Tara, who was now sitting at the foot of the bed. She could see the pain on my face, and I'm sure she could tell that what I was going to say wasn't going to be good.

"Val, what is it? What's wrong?" She asked through her building anxiety.

"Tara, I have a plan to get us out of here, but you're not going to like it." I said.

She looked over at Cian who had the same look of pain and concern as me. "Is it really that bad?" She asked through the tears that were beginning to run down her face.

"I'm not going to lie to you, Tara. This is going to be hard to watch, but I need both you and Cian right now. You need to be strong. We all do." I said as I pushed myself up from the floor and sat down on the bed next to her.

I slowly put my arm around her neck, and at first, she pulled away. I could sense she was still harboring hard feelings towards me for leaving her. After a moment she gave in and turned towards me, wrapped both arms around my neck, and cried uncontrollably on my shoulder. It seemed as though she was allowing herself to let go of several years built up emotions. I put my other arm around her and held her tight.

"Tara, I know you're afraid, but I promise that everything is going to be okay." I tried to reassure her.

She sniffled, wrapped both arms around me, and sobbed into my shoulder. I knew this was going to be exceptionally difficult for her, but we were all going to have to just suck it up. Bravery was going to be the only way to get out of this now, especially for me.

The reunion with my sister and Cian has soften me more than I thought it would, but I was exceedingly grateful for our impromptu encounter. It has been so long since I allowed myself to feel, and I had no clue as to how to console my sister. All I could do was hold her, and allow her to release her tears onto my shoulder.

"You're going to have to be exceptionally strong now, Tara." I said to her. "I have been through much worse than was is about to happen to me. I will make it through this, and I promise we will go back home." I tried to reassure her.

"I don't know how to deal with this, Val." She finally said through her tears. "Please tell me what to do." She said as she looked at me through reddened eyes.

"Tara, there's nothing you can do at this point, with the exception of being strong and brave." I said. "Right now this is all up to me. I'm the only one that can get us out of this alive." I said as I brushed the tears from her cheeks.

I knew this was going to be difficult for the three of us, but more so for Tara and Cian. I was going to have to make sure James knew that my target was no longer a threat, but a necessary alliance. I wasn't entirely sure how he would react to them being here, but I was going to convince him one way or another.

I took some comfort in the fact that I had a way out even if I had to kill James. Savanna would be reluctant to help me, but I had a feeling that she would do whatever I asked of her. I took one look at the clock on the nightstand and realized that it was already almost five in the morning. James would be knocking on my door soon, and I needed to figure out how I was going to handle telling him about Tara and Cian.

I took Tara by the shoulders, looked into her eyes, and said, "my associate will be here soon. He is the one who is helping me escape the organization. I haven't told him about you two yet, and he is just as dangerous as I am." I could see the confusion flash across her face, and knew I had to continue. I looked up at Cian as

I said, "I'm going to need you two to stay in the bathroom quietly while I explain everything to him, okay?"

Cian just looked at me and nodded in agreement. I could tell he understood the seriousness of my words and the warning they held. I watched as he walked over to where Tara and I were seated at the foot of the bed, and sat down next to me.

"I have never stopped loving you, Val." He said. "I'm just glad we are finally getting you back." He concluded with a brief half smile.

I released my hold on Tara's shoulders and turned towards Cian. "I thought as much when you guys tracked me down that time. I've stayed away all this time to protect you both." I began. "I couldn't risk anything happening to either of you, and I still fear for your safety."

Cian put his arms around me, pulled me into his chest, and said, "I know that now."

I just sat there taking a sense of comfort from finally being in his arms once more. It was at this moment that I thought through all the years since I ran away from the orphanage that day. I finally allowed all the suppressed emotions to flood through me, and began to cry into Cian's chest.

"I'm so sorry for all of this." I said to him through my sobs. "I never should've left that day. I was just so angry and scared."

"It's okay, Val." He attempted to console me as he tightened his grip. "I'm never going to let go of you again." He added.

Just then Tara leaned over and laid her head on my back. I could feel Cian move one of his arms to put it around her. The three of us just sat there in silence, and allowed ourselves to take comfort in one another.

CHAPTER
FIFTEEN

IT WASN'T LONG BEFORE THERE WAS A KNOCK at the door. I knew exactly who it was and quickly had Cian and Tara go into the bathroom and close the door behind them. Once they were out of sight, I picked up my small nine-millimeter hand gun, pulled the slide back just enough to make sure it was loaded with a round in the chamber, and made my way to the door.

I put my hand on the handle, pushed it down, and slowly opened the door. James stood there with an annoyed look on his face, which was probably due to my slow and deliberate movements. I could see it written all over his face that he knew something was up. I'm sure his suspicions were confirmed when, once he was in the door, I pushed him against the wall and pressed the barrel of the gun into his chest.

"Damn it, Val!" He yelled. "I thought we were past all of this!"

I looked him in the eyes, which was no easy feat since he was slightly taller than I was. "Oh, we are. There's just a couple of things we need to clear up before I put this gun down." I said matter-of-factly.

"Yeah, and what's that?" He asked clearly annoyed and seemingly pissed off.

I couldn't help but let out a smirk as I looked at him. A part of me still took joy in the fact that I had the ability to easily piss people off. It was one of the many traits that I took pride in. I took a moment or two to revel in the moment, until I noticed the look of ill content on James' face, and realized I was pushing him a little too far.

"Enough games, Val. What the hell is going on?" He asked through grit teeth.

"Okay, Okay." I said. "Don't get your panties in a bunch." I half chuckled as I said it. "Come on." I said as I motioned for him to move into the room with the gun.

I walked backwards towards the bed being careful not to turn his back towards me. I couldn't blame him for that one, since this was the second time in the last few days that I pulled a gun on him.

"Don't worry." I said. "I'm not going to shoot you." I tried to reassure him.

"Then put that damn thing away!" He said, clearly frustrated.

"In due time." I replied. "I just need you to understand something first." I said as I sat down in the computer chair, then motioned for him to take a seat on the bed.

Once he was seated, he looked over at me and said, "what the hell has you so on edge?"

I shook my head at him. "I'm not just on edge." I said. "I've recently found out some information on my target."

"I knew that bastard wasn't who he said he was." James replied to my comment.

"It's so much more than that." I began. "James, that man is my family, and the woman that he is with is my sister." I conveyed my new-found information to him.

"You can't really believe that, Val." He said. "You of all people should know that someone will say anything when they are about to die." James said.

The expression on his face seemed to change between one of disbelief, anger, and frustration. I clearly understood what was going through his mind at that moment. Especially since I had the same thoughts when I confronted Cian and Tara in their room. I knew I was going to have to provide more information in order to prove to him that they were not a threat.

"James, I went to their room with every intention of killing them both." I began. "It was then that I was made to understand exactly who they were, and why they came here." I tried my best to make him understand, but could tell my words were falling on deaf ears.

"What the hell is wrong with you?" He asked loudly enough to where his voice almost echoed in the room.

The only solution left was to bring Cian and Tara out into the room. I got up from the desk chair and walked backwards towards the door. No one, not even Cian, knew that Tara and I had matching birthmarks on our wrist. I was going to have to show James those marks in order to prove that what I was saying was true, and not a ruse in order for them to kill us both.

James started to get up from the bed and I stopped him. "Just stay there." I said. "This is the only way to prove what I'm saying is true."

I stopped just in front of the door to the room where I could call out to Cian and Tara. "Okay, come out." I called towards the bathroom.

James spoke up then out of anger. "Are you kidding me!? They've been here this whole time!?"

"Just bear with me, James." I tried to calm him down while still keeping the gun pointed in his direction.

The gun was a necessary precaution because I didn't know

how James would react, and his anger proved my point. It was at that moment that the bathroom door slowly opened. I saw Cian's head protrude from the small opening. I nodded my head indicating that it was safe to come out.

"Val, are you sure about this?" Cian whispered his question.

"It will be okay." I said. I didn't even have faith in the words as I said them.

I glance over at Cian and Tara with a slight look of concern. If this went sideways, I would do everything in my power to protect them both.

"Cian, stay here." I ordered. "Tara come stand behind me. Whatever happens, don't move from behind me, okay?"

Tara nodded her head signaling that she understood, and the look on her face let me know she knew the dangers of what I was asking. I hated putting her in immediate danger like this, but it was unavoidable at this point. My words have fallen on deaf ears, and physical prof was all that was left.

As Tara moved behind me I said, "take the watch off of my left wrist." The watch was rather large with a leather band that had a couple of buckle clasps.

As she did, she whispered in my ear, "I see what you're doing, but what if it doesn't work?"

"Just follow my lead." I replied as I began to move forward towards James.

Tara kept a tight grip on the back of my shirt as we made our way over to where James was now standing impatiently. I could see the frustration still evident on his face. His body became visibly tense and rigid the closer Tara and I got to him. He was clearly on edge, which only made me tighten the grip on my gun as I stopped a few feet away from him.

"James, look at my wrist." I said as I held out my left arm with the inside of my wrist pointed in his direction. "My sister and I have this matching birthmark on our wrists."

I then glanced back at Tara and said, "Tara, show him."

Tara slowly moved her left arm from behind me and brandished the birthmark on her left wrist that looked identical to the one on mine. You could visibly see her arm shaking from nervousness and fear as she held her arm there next to mine.

James glanced down at our matching birth given tattoos then looked at me with softened eyes. His body language began to change as he relaxed his stance a little and lowered his arms to his sides. He almost a look of awe as he just stood and stared at me then at Tara, who's head slowly moved from directly behind me to just over my left shoulder.

"How can this be?" James asked when he finally spoke after several minutes of just standing there staring.

"They found me. Well, they came up with this whole get together in order to get me back, unaware of my own plans." I replied as I loosened the grip on my gun a little.

"So, what do we do now? If you don't go through with our plan, the organization will not stop until you're dead. Not to mention they are now in danger too." He said.

"I've already let them in on our plan, James." I told him matter-of-factly. "They are fully aware of what is about to happen here, and that this has to be done in order for us to get away."

He just looked at me and nodded. I could see that my reputation was clearly preceding me in this case. I was always known for being well prepared for any situation, and able to come up with multiple plans in case anything went wrong. I had a knack for being able to dance my way, for lack of a better word, around any situation or problem. Maybe that's why I've been able to survive for so long in this game.

"Shall we begin then?" James asked.

"Let's dance." I said as I pushed Tara back a little, spread my arms out, and bowed towards him with a smirk on my face.

I looked back at Tara and motioned for her to move back over to where Cian was still standing by the door. "No matter what happens, you two stay over there." I told both of them.

Just as I looked back at James he surprised me with a right hook to the jaw. I fell to one knee and caught myself on the foot of the bed. It was then that I heard Tara gasp aloud in horror. I tried my best to warn them of the brutality that was going to ensue. I hardly had a chance to regain my senses before James was on me again landing seemingly heartless blows to my face and body.

After a about ten minutes or so of him releasing some tension on me, he stood up and took a couple of steps back. "I know you have more fight than this, Val." He said.

I slowly pushed myself up from the crumpled position I was in on the floor. I straightened my legs, and began to stand myself up. I took one look up at him, put my left hand to the corner of my mouth, wiped the blood that had begun to dribble down my chin on the back of my hand, and grinned.

"Is that the best you've got?" I asked as I lifted my hands into a defensive position resembling that of a form of martial arts, and shook my head from side to side to shake off the buzz from being hit.

James clenched his fist and swung at my head once again. I quickly ducked my head allowing his punch to fly over me. It was then I took advantage of his open left side, and landed a hard jab just under his ribs. He let out a loud grunt, then took another swing with his right hand aiming at my left side. I tucked my elbow into my side and prepared to absorb the impact of his punch.

I allowed my body to move as his fist collided with me. I could hear Cian and Tara quietly cheering me on in the background even though they knew I would ultimately lose this fight. I shifted my weight back onto my left foot and took a step to the right a little to gain some advantage over him. I then prepared to send a right hook towards his face. I tightened my fist just as it landed on his cheek to maximize the impact.

As my fist connected with his face, he fell back a few steps and shook his head from side to side. I could already see the welt growing round his left eye.

"Damn, Val!" He said as he rubbed the welt around his eye.

"We have to make it look real, James. You know that." I told him matter-of-factly.

I wasn't expecting the upper cut he dished out at that moment. My body flew backwards and I landed on my back on the floor. The impact of his fist on my chin rocked me a little making me see stars. I rolled over onto my right side, then rubbed my chin with my left hand. I moved my jaw from side to side to make sure nothing was broken. I could taste the iron from the blood in my mouth. I sucked as much blood and saliva into my mouth before spitting it on the floor then stood back up. My legs still felt a little wobbly as James swung at me again. I ducked under his right hook, and landed a solid punch to his ribs.

As my fist impacted his left ribs, I felt a few cracks and knew that a few of his ribs were broken or fractured. He made a loud grunting sound as he let out the air in his lungs. He took a couple of steps backwards as he rubbed his sore ribs with his right hand.

That punch must have pissed him off, because he pulled his gun out of it holster, took a step towards me, then landed a perfect impact to my left temple. This caused me to fall to my knees and made the room turn dark. I fought the urge to pass out while kneeling on the floor in front of James. I could hear the ringing in my ears as every sensation in my body began to black out.

I knew we were getting close to the end of our impromptu fight as James pushed my shoulders which caused me to fall onto my back. He straddled my torso and began to punch my face. First with his left hand, then with his right. My head bobbed back and forth with each impact. Soon I could feel the swelling around my eyes, then the blood slowly working its way down my cheeks and chin.

I could hardly hear Cian as he pleaded for James to stop the onslaught of punches.

"James, I think she's had enough." Cian said.

The punching ceased, and James said, "come help me put her on the bed."

I was pretty much out of it, but could feel two sets of hands on me. One under my arms, and the other under my knees. Cian and James laid me on the bed. I could hear James tell Cian to take Tara into the bathroom and shut the door. I knew what was coming next at that moment.

"You're not going to want to see this next part." James said breathlessly. "She told you what to do after I leave, right?" He asked Cian.

"Yes." Was all that Cian said as he walked away from the bed.

It wasn't long before I thought I heard a door close. I then felt pressure on the edge of the bed, and James whispered into my ear.

"Okay, Val. It's time, so grit your teeth." he said as he pressed his 9mm silencer into the right side of my stomach.

A second or two later the gun went off and all that was left was the searing pain as the bullet ripped straight through my body. I let out wail from the intense pain. I knew this was going to be hard, and I hoped beyond all hope that I would make it through this.

James grabbed my right hand tightly and said, "Val, all I have to do now is take a picture to send to the agency. I wish you luck in whatever you do next my friend. I know it hurts, but you need to lay as still as possible for me right now."

I put my right arm by my side and the left one I eased up and placed it on the pillow next to me. I then turned my head to the left and attempted to lay as still as I possibly could. I could hear the click from James' phone as he took a few pictures. I started to black out as James put his hand on my right shoulder and shook it a little to get my attention. I turned my head towards him and opened my eyes as best as I could to look at the blurry figure standing next to me.

"It's finished, Val." James began. "I really do wish you all the luck in the world my friend." He said as he leaned over and gently kissed my forehead.

CHAPTER
SIXTEEN

THE NEXT THING I KNEW Cian was pressing a towel on the gunshot wound in order to slow the bleeding. James was long gone by then, and I could hear Cian rushing Tara to get all of our stuff out of the room. I could hear the fear in both of their voices as they spoke with one another.

"Is she going to be okay, Cian?" Tara asked with a shaky voice.

"Yes." He replied. "We just need to hurry up and get her to the hospital before she bleeds out." He continued with a forceful tone in his voice.

I was sliding in and out of consciousness, but could hear rustling around the room. I assumed it was Tara gathering all of our things. Not long after that I drifted off and let my body and mind fall beneath the pain. My mind began to wonder off into the past. It seemed like I was sitting in a movie theater alone watching my entire life stream on the big screen.

Cian's light kiss on my lips brought me back to reality. I could feel his arms slid under my knees and just below my shoulders. He gently lifted me off the bed, and I moaned in pain as I wrapped my right arm around his neck. I did my best to keep pressure on the towel with my left hand as he carried me over to the door. Tara opened the door and held it open for Cian to walk out into the hallway with me.

Cian and Tara walked quickly down the hall towards the back elevators that went directly to the parking garage. Once we were in the elevator, I could feel myself fading again. Cian must have noticed my body going limp, and whispered in my ear.

"You stay with us, Val!" He sounded distressed. "We need you, so don't you dare leave us. Do you hear me?" He asked with a shaky voice as he shook me a little in his arms.

This was enough to send a sharp pain from my stomach to my brain, and wake me back up. I did my best to look up at him and tried to put a smile on my face. I'm not entirely sure that my facial expressions complied with the emotions I was attempting to portray.

"I'm not going anywhere." I tried to say to him. The only thing that came out was a gurgled whisper.

He leaned down at that moment, put his lips on my forehead, and kissed me. "I love you so much, Val. I'm never letting you go." He told me with a concerned smile on his face.

I have to admit that through all that I've faced over the years since leaving Cian and Tara, my heart melted a little in my chest at the fact that they never gave up on finding me or loving me. I have been so hard hearted over the years. I had to be in order to do the work I had to do for the agency. You can't have a soft heart when it comes to killing someone. Each life I took over the years tore a hole in my soul that will take a lifetime to mend. Being a professional killer isn't something you can just walk away from and forget about.

It wasn't long before the elevator doors opened and we stepped into the garage. It was already twilight outside, and the only light in garage was coming from the lamps overhead. I closed my eyes again, but heard Tara talking to Cian.

"Stay here." She said. "I'll go get the car. I'll only be a minute."

I could hear the quick patting of her tennis shoes as she ran in the direction of their car. I'm not entirely sure how long Tara was gone. I believe I must have passed out from the pain again. The next thing I knew Cian was helping me into the back seat of an SUV. Tara gently held my head as I limply sank onto the dark leather seat. Cian lifted my legs enough to slide into the back seat with me.

He gripped my left hand with his, and pressed as gently as he could on the towel covering the gunshot wound on my stomach. I winced and moaned as he pressed down on the towel. I could feel myself drifting as if I was floating on the air. I knew this was from the blood loss and knew I had to make myself hold on.

"Don't worry, Val. We'll be at the hospital in no time." Cian said. "Just hold on!"

"How's she doing, Cian?" I heard Tara ask with a clear sound of worry in her voice.

"Just get us to the hospital." Cian replied forcibly.

I knew they were worried about me and the situation. I hated that they were put into this situation. I never wanted them to see this, or even experience this part of my life. Don't get me wrong, I'm glad they are here with me now. This was just something I wanted to save them from. No one should ever see what I just went through, especially family.

"Tara, we need to hurry." Cian called out worriedly. "She's losing too much blood. I think she's starting to fade back here."

"We're almost there, Cian. I'm going as fast as I can!" Tara replied.

My body was starting to feel cold, and I couldn't see anything despite opening my eyes. I felt my way down my body with my right hand and placed it on top of Cian's right hand, which was holding onto the towel. I did my best to speak at that moment.

"C...Cian?" I attempted to say. My words came out in a gurgled whisper. "I..I'm c..cold."

He let go of my left hand, and a moment later began to awkwardly place a blanket over me. "I know." He said while adjusting the blanket. "Please just hold on!"

I must have passed out at that moment because the next thing I knew I had doctors and nurses surrounding me. I could hear someone asking what happened as someone was cutting my shirt off. It almost seemed as though there were a million people surrounding me. I had nurses pressing gauze onto the gunshot wound, someone was placing a needle into my arm. I assumed they were drawing blood at that moment.

I could feel them preparing me for a breathing tube that would be placed down my throat. Before long I was completely out. They put medication into the IV in my arm to paralyze me and knock me out so they could place the breathing tube down my throat. As I began to drift off from the medication, I could hear Cian whispering in my ear.

"You're going to be okay. You're a fighter, so just keep fighting and stay with us." He said. "Do you hear me? Don't you dare leave me!"

I gave in to the effects of the medicine and let my eyes to close, it was then that everything went dark. I was in a deep enough sleep that there were no dreams or visions of the past. I'm positive that Cian stayed by my side until they rushed me to surgery. This whole situation reminded me of just how much I love him. I honestly don't even remember why I left them in the first place.

I'm not sure how long I was out of it from the medication. I tried to open my eyes, but my eyelids felt like ten pound weights each time I attempted to lift them. After a few moments I was able to open my eyes enough to see that Tara asleep in the chair across the room. I tried to move my head, but when I did, I felt a tug around my mouth. It was then that I started trying to move my fingers, and lift my hands.

Cian must have been sitting next to the bed holding my hand, because the next thing I knew he was squeezing my left hand. I cut my eyes to the left as far as they possible could, then I saw him slowly stand up and leaned over the bed. He gently kissed me on the forehead.

"Don't try to speak or move your head. You still have a breathing tube." He spoke gently into my left ear. "I'll see if I can find a nurse."

Before I knew it, he was out of my line of site. I could then see Tara stirring in the hospital chair next to the far wall. She then fluttered her eyelids, rubbed her eyes with the backs of her hands, and looked right at me. I raised my hand to let her know I was finally awake, and she slowly raised herself up from the chair, stretched, and walked towards my bed.

"Val, I'm so glad you're okay!" She said as she attempted to lean over the bed while trying not to press on all of the tubes and wires covering and hanging from my body. She finally managed to give me a light hug, and kissed me gently on the cheek. "I've missed you so much."

She sat down in the chair next to the bed where Cian had been seated. She then took hold of my left and, brought it to her lips, and kissed the top of it gently. I suddenly began to feel the stabbing pain from my right side. I took my right hand and began to feel around on the bed for the button for the pain pump. Tara must have seen my hand patting around on the bed.

"What's wrong, Val?" She asked.

All I had to do was raise my finger and point at my side. She quickly understood and picked up the button and pressed it. It wasn't long before I had a dose of morphine flowing through my veins. It was hard to fight the drowsiness that followed once the medicine began to take its effect.

Cian and a nurse walked into the room shortly after that. The nurse began her work by checking my vitals, the IV, the ventilator, and finally the catheter bag hanging on a hook at the foot of the bed. She also took a moment to check the drainage tube sticking out of my side from the gunshot wound.

"Well." The nurse began. "Your vitals, as well as your oxygen levels look good. Are you ready to get that tube out of your throat?" She asked.

I couldn't shake my head so I just blinked at her. She nodded in response then touched Cian's shoulder. She and Cian then walked out of the room. I hoped that I wouldn't be in here much longer. I really wanted to get as far away from this city as possible just in case the agency wanted to make sure that I was truly dead.

It wasn't much longer before Cian, the nurse, and the doctor walked into the room. They all made their way towards my bed. Cian stopped at the foot of the bed while the doctor stood next to me on the right side, and the nurse moved over to the left side.

The doctor looked at me and said, "Okay, I'm going to unplug your breathing tube from the ventilator to see how well you are breathing on your own."

I blinked my eyes at the doctor a couple of times to let him know that I understood. He then put one hand on the tube that was hanging out of my mouth, and wiggle the connector tube from the breathing ventilator off.

"Okay." He said. "I want you to take a couple of breaths for me."

I looked him in the eyes and did as he requested. I could not have been more ready to get this tube out of my throat. I was ready to speak and give some instructions to Cian and Tara.

"Very good." He said. "It looks like you're ready to get rid of this thing." He smiled at me as he said that last part.

He then looked at the nurse connected a syringe to the small tube connected to the breathing tube. She looked at me and said, "I'm going to raise the bed some."

As the head of the bed raised up I tightly gripped the sheets and blanket that were covering my body from the waist down due to the pain. I knew deep down that it wouldn't take me long to get used to the pain from the gunshot wound, or the surgery afterwards. I wanted more than anything to get out of here.

After the bed was at an adequate height, the nurse took a small suction tube and put it inside of the breathing tube in order to get rid of any secretions that may have been in there. The nurse then sucked the air the air out of the breathing tube cuff.

The doctor then looked at me and said, "I need you to take a deep breath, then breath out as hard as you can for me as I pull the tube."

At that moment, the doctor firmly gripped the tube and began to pull it out of my throat and mouth. Once the tube was out I began coughing. I saw a look of concern flash across both Cian and Tara's face, then heard the doctor reassure them that it was normal and part of the process.

The nurse moved away from the bed in order to throw the tube and syringe into the red biohazard trash bin. Tara quickly took her place by my side and took hold of my hand once more. I turned my head towards Tara and gave her a smile to let her know I was okay. I knew she was, and had been worried sick about me. I was just happy about being one step closer to getting out of here and being on my way back to Ireland.

I raised my free hand and motioned for something to use to write with and on. Cian quickly picked up a small dry erase board and marker; then he placed it on my legs. I wrestled my hand away from Tara and pulled the cap off of the marker. The only thing I could think to write was:

Thank you! I love you both!

Cian and Tara looked at each other then looked at me. It was almost in unison when they said, "love you too, Val."

Those words were like sweet music to my ears. It had been far too long since I've heard anyone tell me they loved me, or that I've ever said that to anyone else for that matter. There are no words to describe the joy I feel at this moment. Even through the pain, I had no choice but to smile at this point in my life. I couldn't imagine anything better than having my baby sister and Cian here with me right now.

A couple of hours passed and I was finally able to muster the ability to whisper rather than having to write everything down. I shifted slightly in order to adjust myself to a more comfortable position on the bed. It was then that a searing pain shot through my torso. I clinched my teeth and took in a sharp breath as the pain went straight through my body.

"Val? Are you in pain?" Cian asked.

"Do I need to get the nurse?" Tara retorted.

I couldn't even answer. Before I knew it Tara was out of the room and I could hear her calling for a nurse in the hallway. It was hardly a minute later when Tara returned with a nurse in tow.

"What's your pain level?" The nurse asked.

I slowly sucked in a breath and whispered, "eight."

The nurse turned towards the door and walked out. A moment

later she returned with a syringe. She twisted the tip of the syringe into a port on the IV tube and slowly pushed plunger of the syringe injecting the medication directly into my IV.

"This will make you sleepy, but will help with the pain." She said. "Let me know if you need anything else." She concluded as she gently put her hand on mine.

It wasn't long before I began to feel the effects of the medication flood through my body. My eyes were beginning to feel heavy, and it was as if I was seeing a kaleidoscope of colors when I closed my eyes. Cian had one of my hands while Tara had a hold of the other. I gently squeezed their hands in mine before drifting off from the effects of the strong pain medication.

I must have been out of it for several hours, because by the time I woke up it was dark outside with the exception of the soft glow from the lights in the parking lot. I looked over to the left and silently watched Cian sleep in what seemed like an uncomfortable position in the chair next to my bed. His arms were dangling off the sides of the armrests, his head was drooped forward with his chin resting on his chest, and his legs were half bent but still stretched out. I couldn't help but crack a smile at the site of him sitting there like that.

I tried to move my right hand, but realized it was pinned down by Tara who had fallen asleep with her head resting on my arm. She felt the slight movement as the muscles tensed in my arm, and her head popped straight up as if it was shot from a gun. I quickly raised my finger to my lips to keep her quiet.

"Are you okay?" She whispered.

"I'm fine." I replied. "I just want to get out of here already." I grunted as I shifted a little in the bed.

She took a hold of my hand, leaving hers underneath mine, then placed her other hand on top. "We'll be back home soon,

Val." She began. "You just need to heal some more before you are able to get onto a plane."

I gave her a cheap smile and rolled my eyes in response to her comment. I then looked her in the eyes and said, "Tara, I'm so sorry I left you all those years ago. A day did not go by that I didn't think about you."

"It's okay, Val." She began as tears welled in her eyes. "I was angry with you for so long after you left, but I understand now why you felt like you had to go."

"I just felt for so long that everything that happened with mom and dad were my fault. I felt like I should have done more to help them, or at least mom." I said as a tear made its way down my cheek.

Tara put her hand on my face and wiped the tear from my cheek. She then placed her hand back on top of mine. "Val, there was nothing you could do. If you hadn't come upstairs and hid with me when you did…" She began to cry. "I wouldn't have you here with me now."

I looked at her with a fresh pain in my heart. The memory of the day our parents died was almost more than I could handle right now. I just looked her in the eyes and said, "we are going to be just fine, Tara."

ABOUT THE AUTHOR

I AM THIRTY-SIX YEARS OLD. I have been writing since learning about poetry in middle school. I wrote my first poem while in the seventh grade, and have been writing short stories and poetry since. I finally found my love for writing fiction while taking a creative writing English class while in college.

I decided to write about an Irish female assassin after finding out that some of my family was from Ireland. My hope is to give my readers a way to escape the monotony of life by living through the eyes and emotions of my characters.